Tales of the Out
& the Gone

Tales of the Out & the Gone

Amiri Baraka

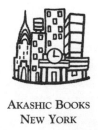

AKASHIC BOOKS
NEW YORK

This is a work of fiction. All names, characters, places, and incidents
are the product of the author's imagination. Any resemblance to real
events or persons, living or dead, is entirely coincidental.

Published by Akashic Books
©2007 Amiri Baraka

ISBN-13: 978-1-933354-12-5
ISBN-10: 1-933354-12-7
Library of Congress Control Number: 2006923115

First printing

Akashic Books
PO Box 1456
New York, NY 10009
info@akashicbooks.com
www.akashicbooks.com

To my wife Amina

Table of Contents

Introduction

What should be obvious in these tales are the years, the time passing and eclipsed, the run of faces, events, unities and struggles, epochs, places, conditions, all gunning through and fueling them. Tales are stories—I like the old sound to it, *tale*. A story (where we have stored something) can be from anywhere and talk of anything. Like Williams said, sometimes memory explains itself as a newness, a future revelation.

But tales, as my mother called my frequent absences from the literal, are not only straight out of my own orally recorded perpetrations, but have a literary stature from Pushkin, de Maupassant, Poe, Dumas, Kafka, Sembène, Bradbury, &c., a parade of awesome presences, themselves *tails*, of eras and assemblages of great thoughts and feelings. What is left of what has left. What my grandfather used to call "the last part of the chicken to go over the fence."

Does this have anything to do with Pin the Tail on the Donkey? It depends on who that ass be! We aims to be democratic, even in our registrations of where we been, is, and going. So there is dim ol' rats and real public coons featured throughout.

Mao sd that "works of literature and art, as ideological forms, are products of the reflection in the human brain of the life of a given society." These tales confirm that. Ideological but also material, to whatever extent the time, place, and condition of our own lives are rendered by our understanding, our perception, rationale, and use of everything we are or that surrounds the inside and the outside of us.

So many of these tales would be juiced-up journalism if I did not think they needed to be something else to be fully grasped. The earliest tales in this book fit that, with their takes on (& almost at the time of) the interior of a social movement.

The slightly gnarled pinpoints of great human struggles raging everywhere across the planet! The trials and errors, attempts, failures, and successes of that period. Told, or half-told, or enhanced, by each succeeding level of knowledge that I was able to fully navigate. So there are sounds and colors and surfaces, as well as images and hard edges and impressionistic recallings. Some emerging philosophical constructs. There is also, at the optimal curtain calls, some real information, some actual use provided.

In specific contexts, anything can be *Out!* Out of the ordinary. So that even the most advanced of us who struggled against racism and imperialism could be called, and sometimes were called, *Out!* Just as we might call some artist, like Thelonius Monk or Vincent Smith or John Coltrane, *Out!* Because they were just not where most other people were. So that is aesthetic and social, often both at the same time.

There are "real" events and events taken from reality and enhanced with the spirit of the thing itself. That's why in the "south" of the world, the bird sits on top of the wise man's head—the soul, the spirit—whether Bantu or Cherokee. When we were told that Osiris, the Djali, raises the sun each day with song and verse, we learned that this is the function of art—to give us light, to let us fly, to let us imagine and dream, but also to create, in the real world.

The stories become tales when they can give us a sense of a less fully experienced dimension to what is.

The "War Stories" in this book's first section are, for the most part, taken from a life lived and experienced, from one kind of war or another. It could be the USAF in Puerto Rico, it could be the later Greenwich Village skirmishes, the Black Liberation Movement, or the Anti-Revisionist Communist Movement (we used to call it). Or what became post- all that. Or it could even be a transmogrification of what happens when people cannot stand reality, perhaps because it is too *accusing*, and so try to duck out on it, but wherever they try to hide, it is right there waiting for them.

What happens to us literally is never obvious altogether. The smashing of the Black Nationalist paradigm of the '60s happened in a number of ways, obvious and un. There are parables here, just like they told us in church. War stories can be tales of what happened "back in the day!" But there are concrete results of real life that have or have not happened, or might have happened or might yet happen, or even metaphorical descriptions of different kinds of life conflicts that move us, whether we can speak of them or not.

The "Out" is out, even if in plain sight. Though it would not have to be. The "Gone" could be seen or unseen or obscene. But even farther "Out," crazier, wilder, deeper, a "heavier" metaphor, a deeper parable. We'd say that's "way out."

(At Howard we were so hip we wd say, "That's way," meaning, "That's way too much," exceedingly hip, super wise. Like a cat we called "Smitty from the City" who when he entered the room addressed us all as "CATS, CATS, CATS," and we sd among us that Smitty from the City was, indeed, way too much.)

The act of imagining is the root of creation. I brought that with me as I grew. I cd imagine my ass off. Sometimes my parents wd try to whip it literally off for such imagining. I told my teacher once that I was late for school because I had to feed the snakes my parents kept in the basement. Little knowing the wench wd come and investigate.

So to tell the whole story of this place, there has to be room to imagine what it means as well as what it seems to be, since all of that is what it is. And this is the shining antique surface that makes the tale. I was a lover of these tales, short stories. Richard Wright (*Uncle Tom's Children*), Langston Hughes (*The Ways of White Folks*), Ousmane Sembène (*Tribal Scars*), Isaac Babel (*Red Cavalry*). All of Kafka's *Outness*.

Earlier, I was a teenage science fiction reader. An *avid*, like they say, reader. The first story I ever published, called "The Cat," as a senior at Barringer High School in Newark, had merely the humming of metaphor made mystical. But from Ray Bradbury's *The Martian Chronicles*, and science fiction from writers like Heinlein, van Vogt, Asimov, Clarke, and the annual sci-fi anthology. Plus the mysterious stories that the radio was hip enough then to offer; remember ESCAPE (with Mussorgsky's *Pictures at an Exhibition* as its theme song), which did the wilder stories by Cheever, H.G. Wells, and many more? All these sources molded my taste for the Out & the Gone. The merely humdrum quickly bored me, the tale had to have some *weirdness*.

The stranger and more science fiction–like that the tales might seem, I hope they still carry a sense of what needs to be addressed and even repaired in the "real world." Octavia Butler and Henry Dumas, though more my contemporaries, yet gone (really) already, carry this kind of social presence, like a hymn of clear morality, in their works. We see what they love and what they hate, what they think ugly and what they think beautiful, as if addressing themselves directly to Mao's dicta in the *Talks at the Yenan Forum on Art & Literature* (1942).

That is not simply my analogy, but a historic litmus analysis for any art.

Sartre sd if you say something's wrong in the world and you don't know what it is, that's art. On the other hand, if you say something's wrong in the world and you do know what it is, that's social protest. At least that's what our enemies say. Fuck them!

Amiri Baraka
The Last Poet Laureate of New Jersey
Newark, NJ, 5/11/06

War Stories

New & Old

The debate was short and sour. Acrid. Unsunny. Though a vein of humor eased through it. It began after three years away from the organization. Conrad faced Pander with the proposition that he, Pander, was an opportunist. That he would come up and criticize operations to others, but say nothing to people's faces.

Pander huffed and puffed through his opened nostrils. A flush of red thru his brown face, fattened by studentdom come late in life.

As revolutionaries, black nationalists, he and Conrad had been together as part of a larger being, World Insurrectionists. W.I. But a silent and tightly focused split sent Conrad, as one suborganization head, off with his folks in another direction. There had almost been a shoot-out on a southern campus between W.I. people and the breaking-away Liberation Afrikan Front. L.A.F. people.

Pander had been where in that? Had he already left W.I., or what? During that period or a little earlier, Simba, the leader-teacher, apparently had Pander cracked across the skull and driven out with his running partner, Big Yellow Jerome, who's now a City Hall dope dealer. Cleaner. Wabenzi (the tribe that drives in the Mercedes Benzes). The whole story on that. The head whipping. The flight. Accusations that

Pander was "an agent who pushes pills" inside the organization. All that remains unclear. Or too clear.

Except Simba got worse, from the strain of revolutionary struggle. Began to swallow too many stay-awake and stay-asleep pills. Became a drowsy ordering vegetable. Amidst the cries for blood, the secret and public capitalist hit men also cried. Amidst internal and external machinations, opportunism—a more exotic withdrawal from the real world. Madness in the smoke of sweet incense. A machine gun set up on a tripod just inside the door of the house. Servants padded in stockinged feet. People pulled in and questioned. Through the fog, conspiracies hatched conspiracies— all fake. Except the real one, that worked.

Conrad gave money to Simba's brother to rescue him, take him to a hospital. The brother didn't even bother to report. Except months later, he explained the obvious: He had failed.

But all this, simply to set the proper pincer of memory and light. Truth moves the faces back and forth. Pander began talking in a rush. "Phrase mongering," he said. Being criticized for behind-the-back criticizing to the R.C. The Right Commies, a group of young, mostly white students calling themselves "multinational workers." About how it shudda been. With thousands of Puerto Ricans ready to rip, boiling outside on the pavement in front of City Hall. Safely indoors, the Nigger Mayor losing weight, oinking like a panicked porker with his little tail curling up under his coat, nailed in place by the way his neck sat, holding up his doofus face. Conrad, the Puerto Rican leaders, and another organization—the Leopards—ran back and forth between City Hall negotiations and the pavement. The crowd had converged from the Puerto Rican ghettoes of the city, El Barrio, to scream at this ugly life. One of their children had been trampled to death by a mounted policeman, trying to stop two Puerto Ricans from shooting crap in the middle of a folklore festival. Two more, both Puerto Rican, died. Shot in the back and the back of the head. The last one pistol-whipped in the face, for good measure.

The negotiators, of course, read and shouted demands, impossible even under the crumbling illusion of bourgeois democracy. And now it was the nigger—a grim fatso who stuffed himself daily with five or six meals, combined into two for austerity. He rode in a Checker cab instead of a Cadillac to give the illusion that he wasn't spending money. He changed mistresses so people who knew the old fat one would be confused because they wouldn't know the new fat one. But they knew both and laughed casually or derisively, depending on whether or not they had a city job.

Police review boards—Amnesty for all the prisoners—A people's investigation team—Expose the causes of the police riot— Free medical care! These were the demands. And the Nigger Mayor acted like the Cracker Mayor, co-collaborators with the dying order. Skin freaks still didn't understand this. "Give him a chance," they said. Though now they couldn't say it to the Puerto Ricans. Or maybe the fools could. Like big outtashape loudmouth Ms. Birdie, in charge of the anti-poverty special-education fund. "These Podaricans is takin' everythin'," she said. A working-class recruit to the petite bourgeoisie, with aspirations from early times.

Conrad told how she sang opera. She was Cio-Cio-San in *Madame Butterfly*, with pink makeup on her dark skin, even on the lips, with white sequined gowns and hair tossed in high piles like frozen custard, Vaseline flavor. She was in training then to play this sorry role, big outtashape loudmouth hard bureaucrat of nigger-shuffle garbage can–eatin' para(meta)dise. "These Podaricans is takin' everythin'." Yeh. Poverty, exploitation, oppression, white feet—now Bignigger feet. They got, truly, everything!

"Whatta I supposed to do about these?" In the middle of Nigger Mayor scowling at being confronted with reality, a rock through his window made his eyes spin like Laurel & Hardy. When we got to the street, the rocks showered City Hall like Robin Hood's arrows. The fat middle-class foolish nigger called to his hoodlums—mostly Italian, but with some young niggers fronting. One, the chief, with a huge 'fro and crimson-and-gold dashiki, had gone to Harvard—N.Y. clean, really. But then the lower-echelon state hit men came on horseback and in squad cars. On foot, the crowd had been walking. Now they rolled, and young dudes waiting for this shit whipped out crowbars and bashed store windows down Main Street, punctuating the sirens. Crisscross, the police cars wheeling, knocking people over. A new technique: high speed, then last minute, wheel around in a sharp turn, bashing the rebels into the sidewalk or up against the building. Conrad and the others, in the middle of the people, jumped to the sidewalk just in time. The cop car smashed one of the Leopards, sideswiped him twenty feet across the ground, but undead. The pigs scrambled out and leaped at his chest, wailing with sticks. Conrad said, "Walk, walk. Slow down. Don't run, just check 'em out."

The beatings went on. The whole of Main Street filled up with new storm troopers. Whites scowling. Blacks peeping. But all almost on the line to kill for the twelve thousand, if they had to.

A roll of poor people running against the shoetops of the mighty, whose blue louses came out from between the toes to beat and maim and murder. Demonstrations would go on, more protests. José Liga, head of the Revolutionary Puerto Rican Communist Organization, Conrad Barker of the L.A.F., Leopard leaders, and community and student groups, held a press conference announcing they would march in the streets—no matter that the nigger weasel downtown had banned it. "Fuck you, weasel!" was their simple rejoinder. And march they did, filling the streets, the downtown, and the park with denunciations of the neocolonial niggers and collaborating Puerto Ricans, the state's pitiful hit men, and the state itself—the instrument of the du Ponts, Mellons, Rockefellers, Fords, &c. It went well. And Pander and his student people were there too, marching with the rest. Standing in the crowd, trying to grin. This was after the meeting, the criticism, the slender memory. The knowledge that even fleeing, reality remains in reality. Were these their class origins? The petit bourgeois thrust at socialist rap. The years of narrow nationalism and polygamous opportunism? Suburban privilege? Or what?

The day Pander arrived with his head split open, red pants, saying he was digging Sly and the F.S. The white boy with him rapped about left opportunism and narrow nationalism. He had thick glasses and Lucky strained to like him because he wanted to be a socialist and abandon his black chauvinism. His hatred of whites. So he described it to Conrad, what the sectarian shoot-out had been, in tones that showed he wanted to deal with these socialists. But Conrad, looking from the back of the truck where he stood waiting to speak, was wondering what Pander and the young white revolutionary Gruen had explained to their people. At the point of the police attack, they shouted to nobody and everybody, "Let's get outta here, we ain't gonna get killed!" and sped away in their three- and four-year-old cars.

Who were these people? And what had their criticism outside City Hall consisted of? Would they help smash the capitalist system? How? Conrad swallowed and got ready to speak "people."

He began, "People, people. We gonna win anyway!"

The crowd agreed and hollered.

February 1974

Neo-American

Goodson readied himself for his big day. Up a little early, shower, read the *Measure* (local paper), glance at the *Times*. Checked specifically the word on the goings-on. Namely, the President of the United States coming to town. And he had the biggest front on it, since he was mayor. The Mayor. (A quick look in the mirror confirmed that it was him thinking about him, and check, any photos handy? Luckily—or as usual— they was right there.)

Touch down: 6 p.m. Streets clear all the way to the hotel. Motorcade convoy. Five hundred overtime cops. Quick call to Chambers. "Roger? Yeh, how's it look? Uh-huh. Uh-huh. OK. Yeh. What about the Ray thing, is that set up? The ACLU? Oh yeh? Fuck 'em. I don't give a shit about their rights, nor those people they got frontin' for them. Yeh . . . Ha ha ha . . . Yeh. OK, check you at noon, huh? OK."

Yesterday, ate, worked a usual day. No, that was his day off. He slept most of the day. Called the office, called Roger. Checked all the preparations. Rode by the hotel where the president would speak. A banquet. Goddamn, a Republican banquet. Thousand dollars a plate. Goddamn Republicans raising a quick million in Finland Station. Be here four hours, tops. He'd talked to the president a couple of times. He had called him Tim.

"How are ya, Tim? How's everything in Finland Station? You're doing quite a job, Tim. Quite a job. Ever think about getting on the team all the way? I mean, leave the jackasses and join the big elephants?"

"I'm on the team now, Mr. President." (Couldn't call him Jer . . .) "Just a different wing of the old bird."

"Wrong wing." They laughed. Plastic cover somewhere, at a press conference just before a press conference. A group of black leaders. A group of mayors from all over. A lunch. Different salads, white wine. Tim burped, caught it in his hands. Fuckin Ray wrote a story about Tim, "Burping for His People." Fuck him. I'm the . . .

Yesterday. No, the day before. Up early, ran around the lake the right way. Seeing these people going uphill the other way, struggling up them hills. Tim went the right way where it was mostly downgrades. This goddamn Sloane there, coming down the wrong way. The goddamn Checker cab made them get the hell off the road. Tim was running around the lake with two policemen riding in front of him in a big Checker cab, rather than the Cadillac that came with the office. The Cadillac would've drawn a little too much fire. This way, a Checker, that's offbeat and looks a little humble, dig?

At City Hall, a lot of Muslims got jobs now too. We give them jobs to be cool with everybody. A little here, a little there. "Just fire Sloane's people wherever you see 'em. Anybody you think is hooked up at all with that Revolutionary Congress, burn 'em! Nowhere, no way!" Tim was screaming at Ethan Montgomery one morning. "These R.C. people are never on time, never there." Some of them were demonstrating against Tim the same morning in front of City Hall. "Then they want to come in here and get paid. I ain't going for that. Burn them niggers."

S.O. Hares, the first black President of the City Council, meets Tim. Gray sideburns tinted red, slightly. (Could dig it if you checked close.) Burned russet wire sunglasses. Light-brown and dark-brown big checked jacket and pebble texture rust pants. "Hey, your boy is burning the hell outta you, Mr. Mayor." He laughs. "Half a one of them goddamn poverty programs is out there too. Ha ha ha." Hares would run next year, the bastard. Next year. He had the Dons to put up the money for him. See, it's a fight between the different groups. But Tim knew he had it made, 'cause he had the biggest group. Gratitude Insurance controlled the whole state. Every major institution and corporation in the state had to check off with or was controlled or heavily influenced by Gratitude. And they had invested early in Tim.

"Me and the people at Grat., Laird Conroy and the rest of the folks, we very tight. But you understand, they're the real controls. What power do I have?" (The rap would change according to who it was.) "The real power is with the economic boys. Laird Conroy is the man." Up in the white marble tower, with Gratitude spelled out in blue steady lights—the first thing the airplanes see.

"The Negro that runs with the Republicans can't get up too tough a head of steam, because Rocky and them know these mostly nigger voters ain't going for no Republican—black or not. But then you got the Cosa Nostra, with S.O. trying to push their luck. If S.O. looks too good, he'll get busted straight out for sticky fingers or a morals charge."

Tim saw Maureen that early evening and they went to New York right after she got off work, for two Gibsons apiece and some pretzels. He was "working late" again. She was a librarian and a real positive step up from Ruthie. Ruthie cried and swelled up in her yellow bulk. But his wife Madeline was hip to Ruthie, and had been for a few years. Ruthie was on the board of everything and was his assistant campaign manager. She was a good campaigner, and pushed the campaign heavy all the time. Talked to a lot of people, sold a lot of tickets, set up a lot of coffee klatches at people's houses. Ruthie knew a lot of people. Plus she was especially in charge of "prone candidate orientation," but had now swelled up to damn near 300 pounds. Big and yellow with flat sticky red lips. She had her boards and titles and a couple of good salaries. What would she need now with Tim? So Tim reasoned, and now slid with Maureen. She woke him up to the *Times Book Review*'s List of Best Sellers. *Jaws. Ragtime. CIA: Coup in America*, the true story of John Kennedy's murder. He got a chance to deal with a couple of pages now and then. *Jaws* was a better movie than book. So would the rest be. Be better as TV programs.

He never missed Roger K. Smith or the Channel 13 weekly news review. It's a heck of a lot of work running a big city. Especially one like Finland Station, with a half-million people—almost 400,000 of them black or Puerto Rican. With a bunch of big mouths floating around on the edge of that, playing like leaders, always stirring some bullshit up.

Like this president thing. The man's just coming here to speak, raise some funds for the Republican Party. So we gotta have a whole lot of demonstrations and bullshit like that, just to build one of these people's names. Tim marched in picket lines. He knew when stuff was on the up and up and when it was BS. *This* was BS. Why? Because the president wasn't going to do anything. There was nothing that could be accomplished by demonstrating in front of the hotel where the president was. What's that gonna do? It ain't gonna get nobody no jobs. *I'll fix these simple niggers tho, they won't even see the president. And he won't see them either—I'll fix them.*

Tim made this statement in the newspaper, and immediately the ACLU and some other bleeding-hearts called him up to protest, saying that they would sue if he violated the democratic rights of the R.C. *By the time that stuff even gets to where somebody will look at it, everything will be got up and gone. Ha.*

By 12:00, the staff meeting began. Reports. The police ready. Five hundred overtime. Cost of $30,000 to the city. "Do the newspapers have that?"

"They got it, alright, and are blowing it all over. And our friends are at it on the radio. The R.C., your friend Sloane, and the others. Putting down the whole business."

"Yeh, but what the hell we gonna do? The president comes—he gotta get security. And the city gotta pay for it. It's a hell of a thing, him a Republican and this city full of black Democrats."

"Most of them not no Democrats, neither," shot in Augie Bond, the drunk PR man.

"But what you gonna do?"

"I ain't no goddamn Democrat either, Boss. You know that." (The staff called Tim *Boss*. He cherished that.) "The bastards at least oughta contribute to the city for the security at a Republican fundraiser. What the hell?"

"Yeh, they oughta, but what will an *oughta* buy?" Rachel Mooney now sat in such a way that the talcum she put on her drawers was visible on the hairs of her upper thigh. Tim smiled and caught another burp, stifling this one completely. They finished the meeting. The usual.

Goodson's collection: old Italians from the former administration, young whites from the Ivy League who wanted to "help" (at 25 Gs a shot), Tim's friends in his "Association" serving as the enforcers of what passed for "policy." These were the only loyalists. Some blacks with high side degrees, mostly from out of town. The young whites and the out-of-town blacks had a quick and consistent turnover. As soon as they got their resumes filled with a year in the jungle counter-insurgency funk, they took off for slicker pastures, wherefrom to sideburn their way into whatever they thought was hip. In the real world, outside the discotheque-like interiors of the new City Hall. (It wasn't new, it just means that now there was Bloods inside; a black bureaucratic elite, complete with Pierre Cardin suits, humpback high heels, beards, sideburns, Mercedes Benzes, Porsches, and Lincoln Continentals—it bugged the boss that he couldn't get one, but he had to give off an image like he wasn't just high in a hog.)

The administration functioned by having people come to work in the city. Most of the good city jobs (most of the real jobs in Finland Station) were held by whites from the opulent suburbs—Livingston, Short Hills, Forest Hills, Essex Fells, Madison. In fact, New Jersey had the second highest per capita income in the United States. But in cities like Finland Station, Newark, Jersey City, Camden, and Trenton, where the niggers lived, the people who came in made the dust and ran back to the suburbs, while the urbs went to the outskirts of town and worked in shoestring factories or auto factories, iron works, paintbrush factories, breweries, and toy factories—when they could get gigs. That's why Tim had to come on not too sparkly. It was bad enough already. Old folks still smiled at him, but some of these loudmouths were beginning to blow their bad breath heavy his way. "Look, I do what I can. What can I do? We just don't have the money. The federal government sends no more money. We do what we can."

But mostly it seemed, especially to the loudmouths including Tim's ex-friend Ray Sloane, like Stevie Wonder's tune, "You Haven't Done Nothin'." And they kept saying that every time Tim surfaced.

"Like when those bitches from Redspear Health Insurance were demonstrating, Sloane brings these goddamn women down through the streets to City Hall. Then, when I went out to dedicate the park across the street, he gets on a bullhorn and starts to shout me down, and sics these freaking women on me. I had to get back inside."

Somebody was passing around red cigarettes with gold filters. "Boss, you want one?"

But sometimes it brushed him further than he

wanted to go. He was there, on top. He knew presidents, kings, and had been halfway around the world. The State Department sent him to Poland to tell those people how black people are really living, so they wouldn't believe the propaganda.

"According to those guys, the Klan's still taking people out they house! But Jesus, I've done something, something any one of these guys would give their left and right nut to do. Me. The Mayor. [Caught it.] And still, you got these jealous-ass niggers wanting to try to show me up. But it won't work. They can't beat me."

The time Jerry Lloyd, the preacher and radical councilman, led students down to City Hall to dump garbage that wasn't picked up in the 3rd Ward, Tim had them busted. He knew them—they'd initially campaigned together in the big push in '70 that sent old Mayor Bucarillo to prison. But "Lloyd was wrong." A couple of black cops got busted that day too, trying to protect the women. Cops arresting cops, white and black cops fighting in the street.

"He was in with that Sloane. That's why he got beat in the elections too. Trying to tear my ass and got his own ass torn."

Also, the AFL-CIO, Teamsters, Democrats, and Republicans backed Lloyd's opponent, "Rip" Dalton. Sloane said he was one of the original Daltons, and came to the council meetings with a bandana around his face so people would be hip to him. S.O. should wear a mask and an all-black suit and big ten-gallon hat. At least then you'd be clearly hip to who and the others there: two liberal blacks—one a college professor on the slightly trembly side, the other an overweight used-to-be-good-guy back in the Civil Rights days, who passionately wanted to be a councilman, and then one day he was, but he'd by then promised his whole 700-pound behind to Tim for backing him. A blushing prostitute, therefore. And five white folks—three ex-cops, a storekeeper, and the wife of a dead man, who got in on his rep and mostly his name.

All the contradictory motions of the place, cross-currents in this here "democracy," where whatever wants to bite you can bite. Its teeth could look like anything; you might even vote for them to bite you. Sloane running it down outside City Hall to the pickets: "Whatever mob wants to bite you. Gratitude owns Tim Fatson. That's Manufacturers Trust and them. Rockefeller owns Jisholm & Bangel and them. Morgan owns them Kennedy-chasing Bloods. The mafia own people like S.O. Hares and Rip-Off Dalton. One mob or another. These politicians are lieutenants, the big ones and the lackies—the small rip-offs peeing on us around here."

Tim listened through the windows. Made himself a cup of tea in front of the big picture windows. The sound boomed in. "That bastard."

Ethan squinted down and Augie made a straight face, trying to joke with Tim about it. "That bastard is gonna bite off more than he can chew one day. Somebody's gonna come runnin' down here to cry how some of them cops blasted him."

Outside: "And what we got here in this town? Niggers in high places, black faces in high places, but the same rats and roaches, the same slums and garbage, the same police whippin' your heads, the same unemployment and junkies in the hallways muggin' your old lady. What is it? What is it? We strained to elect this nigger mayor, and what we got to show for it? Nothing but a burpin' black bastard slippin' his way around the city, sleepin' with fat ladies."

Sloane raved on. Loza laughed, hearing him in the crowd, and noted that the last statement wasn't politically educational. He thought it seemed unprincipled. Too abrasive, he decided. It was not analytical enough.

But Sloane raved on: "It is this system of monopoly capitalism that must be destroyed. The private ownership of the means of producing wealth, the land, the factories, the minerals, the mines . . . These must be controlled publicly and collectively by the masses of people, under the dictatorship of the working class. These black faces ain't enough. It is a system that oppresses us."

"Now the creep is talking like a goddamn commie," Ethan was saying. "Boy, they gonna carry his ass away from here."

There was a line of fifteen policemen on the stairs of City Hall that day as the women from the Redspear sang, with the R.C. people among them urging the singers forward.

After the staff meeting, Tim inspected the hotel setup again, checked out the marked streets of the president's route to the hotel. Talked to the newspapers at a press conference. He thought about Maureen and decided to stop by the library. Call from a phone booth—get her to come to a side entrance. But nobody answered. He pulled off, the car being driven by one of the cops, his bodyguard. And turning the corner, he saw Maureen and his wife, Madeline, standing in front of the library, talking. Madeline still worked for a real estate firm in the area, but it wasn't that close. She wouldn't give up her job—she said they needed to save all they could to get a house in the North Ward or Orange.

He was going to ride on by, but Maureen spotted him and looked, and Madeline turned right away. They both looked. It seemed that the contradiction was going to soon become antagonistic. He waved out the car. Slowed. "Hey, what you all into? I'm on my way to the hotel. You want a lift?" Maureen and Madeline had cars.

"How you doing?" Maureen tried smiling.

Madeline stared. "The hotel?"

"No, thank you," they both said together.

"See you back at the house then. We ain't got a lot of time. It's 3 now—he gets in at 6."

The car ran on, down through traffic. Stopping now at the police station, and checking with Chambers again. There was already a loose cordon being thrown around the general area of the hotel. A snow fence had been erected as well. There was to be an area in which no one was allowed but the police and the eaters at the thousand-dollar-a-plate dinner.

"They say they're gonna sue, Tim, if we don't let them demonstrate. We figure we'll let them demonstrate, but put them in the middle of the park or somewhere, OK?"

"Yeh, what the hell. As long as they can't make no trouble." Really, he meant as long as they can't get in the way of his future motion up the ladder to Colored

Retainer Heaven. If that goddamn McGovern had won, he'd have already made it. Secretary of Housing and Urban Development. A cabinet member. That was the spot. Get cut in on some nice deals that way too, rather than the greasy stuff you had to pick up on the lower level. And that was even a little dangerous now, in these recent post-Watergate years. The take is allowed—everybody there does it. Tim let it roll through his mind. Everybody did that. Nixon did it. But the stuff upstairs is worth the risk. Not this greasy stuff where you got to be connected up with people like Wurlitzer Willie and the rest of the crew. So don't get in the way of the big trip. The big rip.

Sirens turned his head. They were normal for Finland Station every other minute. Sirens howling. It brought to mind the motorcade they would bring the president in with. There was talk all through the halls. And at every stop, people wanted to know and tell and speculate and myth-make.

He spotted Foster Tarasso, the congressman from the Dent District, coming out of the Eldridge Club with his entourage. The club was near his district office. Tarasso was in town for the dinner—all his trips to his district were strictly and only political. Washington was Tarasso's real home. He was the silver-haired orator symbolizing the Italians' rise to semi-respectability in America, when they could keep the friggin' Mafia headlines out of the newspapers and squash those reruns of *The Untouchables*. They exchanged oblique compliments. Tarasso thought Tim wanted his spot. Tim thought Tarasso wanted the HUD spot. Now that Tim had become an official Democrat, the elections in the Finland Station municipal government were non-partisan. Tarasso felt a little safer, but still had to watch his back. Tim had to watch his front. They discussed the dinner and the demonstration. The fact of the assassination attempts. The tight security. The newspapers bombing Tim on the $30,000 being spent to protect the president. Tarasso had a young girl, his legislative assistant, in the car. She waved and kept talking to the other couple sitting in there. Tarasso's law partner or his companion, another legislative assistant, or secretary, or reporter, or what have you. Tim wondered what they looked like naked.

They made the last stop and went back to the house. Madeline was already there. He picked up his brown tuxedo with the tossed ruffle shirt and neat velvet tie. The schedule indicated to pick up the convoy and arrive at the airport by 5:15. Air Force One would land at exactly 18:00 hours and the motorcade would proceed—after a briefing with the Secret Service men—directly to the hotel. Fifty miles an hour all the way.

Madeline was dressing. She spoke when he came in and said nothing afterwards.

He began to take off his clothes. "You about ready?"

"Yeh."

"How long you been home?"

"Long enough to be almost ready."

A slight edge, barely rising. He was quiet, pulling his socks and suspenders out of the drawers. Emptying his pockets on the table. Making sure his cologne was out. And that he had some money in the clip. And all his ID cards. He turned to go into the bathroom and Madeline was standing there with her long skirt on, but her top in her hands, wearing her brassiere.

She said, simply, "If I catch you with that woman, I'm gonna kill both yo asses."

"What?" The radio was playing. WDNL, Soul Radio. Millie Jackson had come on, talking about another woman. That's what had set her off, the dumb-ass song. "What you talking about?"

"You know what I'm talking about. My girlfriend saw your car down there at that library two or three times. I didn't know that fat yellow bitch was in there. You just got rid of one fat yellow bitch. I shoulda known why. To pick up another one. But I'm telling you, Tim, I'll waste both yo asses." She turned and went out the door.

"What?" He started saying some other things, but convinced nobody in the apartment since only the two of them were there. They had no children. He'd had some by another marriage, but they were grown. He kept talking.

Madeline shouted back, "Yellow fat-ass bitch! You like them yellow-ass fat women, why you marry me then?"

Madeline was a brown-ass fat woman, chocolate-sweet when grooving, burning fire when crossed. It passed through Tim's mind. *Yeh, why?* The yellow streak was on him—*in* him. He was himself a fat yellow person. It was 4:30. He had to rush into the bathroom. They said nothing else until it was time to go out together. He said, "You always hooking me up with somebody. Why pick her?"

"*You* picked her, not me." Madeline went down the

front stairs. It was a small white wooden house. A two-family house, the top floor occupied by Madeline's sister and her husband, again kept up from the old days to maintain the image, though arrangements were already being made for a house in the country. You couldn't be moving around all these people—the world's petit bourgeois and the big boys too—without that life producing its own projections. Its notions that had to be fulfilled, its wobbly ideas and grand designs.

The turbulence of the Civil Rights black power decade was what brought Tim Goodson to this spot, yet the spot was ultimately something which was that decade's opposite. Goodson had marched in front of Barton High to demand jobs for black contractors, and was in the picket lines around the proposed 200-acre medical school, which was a cold-blooded attempted rip-off of black people from out of the area to stave off the realities of what black power meant at that point. It was a gag to get rid of black voters.

He was a part of the Civil Rights movement, the thrust that hooked up with Martin Luther King pressing for the black vote all over the South, and the young SNCCers who followed that path, the struggle for democratic rights which boiled most fiercely in the land-base of the Black Nation, the black belt South. The fire of Malcolm had emerged then to raise the struggle to still higher levels with the true voice of the working people—aside from the motion that the black bourgeoisie could direct, the good preachers of SCLC representing the other preachers and teachers and doctors and lawyers. It's why the student hook-up was exactly cool, the middles and upper-middles of the Black

Nation. Yet the motion was a mass motion. The millions with their might opposed the segregation and discrimination, the white-only apartheid that finally even the big boys themselves saw was passé, that if they wanted to get on top of the world market as almighty U.S.A., the Camelot of the world, then they also had to cool out them old relationships. Stuff had to be modernized, Jimmy. Dig? Old Bull Connor's just out of whack with the times, JFK could have remarked coolly to himself in the oval room, posing for a picture with the big six leaders and Rabbi Prinz and Walter Reuther.

The motion then—the democratic rights, the voting, equal access—finally to where, when we stood up on the cars in the middle of the street screaming we had won, we had won, and hoisted fat-ass Tim in the air, we had won. Yeh, as if the lost democratic revolution that the KKK counterrevolution squashed after reconstruction had been completed, and we were equal in America, 'cause now we had "power." It is only the middle class that could think of that, Sloane would yell at the crowd. The people need control of the economy of this country. The land, the factories, the mineral wealth, all the people, together . . .

Until it became clear that Tim was *them*, the owners—a "new way into things." That nothing had changed but the cover it wore. The new was niggers, or whoever is demanding what. A little special elite of them set up to run the ex-colonies. Yet . . . blood in the streets, squashed faces under tank treads. A woman thrown against the wall, shot in the throat, her baby slips from her arms. We watch gagging in the jail through bars, while the carbine rings like a sweet bell.

Lead fists against the National Guard trucks. They hide like the coward faggots they are.

Nothing had changed.

Tim was in the car with Madeline hunched over to one side. There were two police in the car now. Black police members of the Quixotes—a black cop fraternity sworn to protect the mayor, especially from white police. They moved toward the airport. It was just after 5:00. And as they turned to go across the downtown bridge, two other police cars picked them up. In one was Roger Chambers, the Harvard grad who was Tim's political appointee as Police Director. Roger wore dashikis on Saturdays and was one of the only police directors with a beard. He liked to throw out a Swahili greeting at the militants when they came to bug him. He'd also turn on Herbie Hancock in the background to cool them out. The Cosmic Echoes if they got *too* far out.

In another car was the black Superintendent of Schools, with his special wine-aged briar pipe ($750) and black Algerian tobacco. The Chief Judge of the Municipal Court, also black. With black watch, tartan dinner jacket, and long Dunhill cigarettes, looking frantically at his watch because he still had to call his woman Ida to see that she met him at the door exactly at 7:00. His wife would watch the proceedings on television, read her Bible, and go to bed.

In various cars, they arrived at the airport, and finally coming to the set that night would be the entire crew of WaBenzi (Swahili: the tribe that drives the Mercedes Benzes), the Blood Elite. Got over from the black muscle of the '60s. The sister who was Executive Director of the City Hospital butcher shop, the head of the anti-poverty program (another sister). The business administrator, another Yale Law School graduate in a B.B. suit, natch. S.O. and his orange sideburns running with the Welfare Chief (she was an old head that had survived from the days when whites ran City Hall, and now she gloried in the coming together of survivors of the last epoch and the rulers of this). President of the Board of Education, a dude who wore cultural nation-alist talismans over his blue Barney's suits. He had a red, black, and green pick he did his 'fro with too.

Along with the whites in the administration, country politicians, big-wigs from the Republican Party, and their nigger-figures as well, including their candidate for mayor: a "black" slumlord who was attacked by Sloane and the R.C. the year before because two black children died of lead poisoning in one of his $175/month dungeons from eating the old paint off the peeling walls.

The dribble of banter rode around bubbly. Wax words oozed. Lies, conjectures, postures, puny puns. Many had a last drinky-boo at the bar inside the airport before striding out, a comfortable triumphant little group, the in-it politicos of the state, and the po-lice, troopers, FBI, secret police, and more porters than the airport ever had. They all waited. On television, the head of the NAACP could smile—there were blacks "ever-where," including Tim, there, in the front line, with Governor Rose, the President of Gratitude (an old-school friend of the vice president's), the Chairman of the N.Y.–N.J. Port Authority (a public corporation), the Republican State Chairman, the Republican Senator Cod, several county leaders.

They stood expectant as the door opened and the

big-headed, empty-faced moron who fronted off for the corporate dictatorship that ran America slid down the stairs, out of the plane.

Roger Chambers and his chief were briefing the Secret Service men as the motorcade began to shape up. The president was reaching the end of the line of people waiting for their hands to be shaken. The television was recording it all for posterity. There were about six or seven college-aged whites on the street outside the airport, but cordoned away from where the president's motorcade would run, carrying signs, accusing him of being *The Chief of Imperialism*. They screamed at the cars as they pulled out and drove up the ramp they couldn't get close to. Some other people waved at the line of vehicles and talked excitedly.

As planned, the motorcade hit the bridge at fifty miles an hour, and the systematically timed lights blinked green straight ahead. The police sirens raised their customary wail and would have raised heads other places, but just made a slight dent in the consciousness of the black, Puerto Rican, and blue-collar white "Finns," who assumed it was merely the usual crime-busters action that went on in that town twenty-five hours a day. Though some had read the papers, listened to the radio, and stood at the curb looking at the motorcade. They waved. They called. Some gave it the finger. A few Puerto Rican teenagers at Britton Street said, "Fuck yooooo," as the motorcade passed.

The R.C. had reached the downtown area where the demonstration was scheduled about twenty minutes before the president touched down. They were met by the tactical squad, who said they would not be allowed in the area specified in the demonstration permit application. Just as Goodson had said in the newspapers, the police were going to keep them from getting too close to the president. "He won't see them, and they won't see him," is the way he put it.

Sloane cursed the police, said they were gonna get their asses sued for this violation of the people's democratic rights. The police said OK, and turned away. The long line of demonstrators, each with a different sign unfurled, walked around the outside of the cordoned-off area, chanting. "President and Rocky eat thousand-dollar dinners/while the people are exploited by the capitalist system." Over and over again, waving the signs. They also had a big banner they carried with four main slogans: *Capitalist Lieutenant Ford Vetoes the People's Needs! Jobs, Not Imperialist Wars! Victory for the National Liberation Struggle Is a Victory for the Working Class! Support the Peoples of the World Struggle against the Super Powers!* Young people got on their line of about 200. They talked about Ford and Rocky, about the Vietnam and Cambodian Wars, about unemployment, lay-offs, budget cuts. Police were heavy in and around the park. Disguised as vendors, drunks, passersby, along with the Secret Service. Unobtrusive, like an alligator in a dinner jacket. There was a new ring of people forming around the cordoned-off area to watch. A couple of smaller groups of demonstrators, some carrying signs saying *Rollback the prices!* Obviously suburbanites who wanted to buy more stuff with their loot.

America in the 1970s, in the pit of depression called recession. One out of every four blacks unemployed, Finland Station the gut end of that. Thirteen percent of the whole nation unemployed, and in Finland Station it soared to thirty percent, fifty percent of the youth. And at nights there were more muggers on the streets than regulation folks. Sometimes the muggers mugged each other. Other times, they would mug police decoys, which they scattered all over the bleak slum, disguised as disguised cops.

The cries about the thousand-dollar-a-plate dinner hit home with a lot of the working people walking near the park, just coming from shopping, and even some of the people who were crowded around the outside perimeter hoping to see a glimpse of power. The line went from one chant to another, and circled back and forth on the perimeter where they were permitted to march. It was very late Saturday afternoon, turning to early evening. The shoppers were spreading after coming out of the bargain basements. They stopped to look at the signs and listen to the words being shouted at them.

Who's that? What's that for? That's Sloane and them. Uh-huh. What they talking about now? President—you know he's supposed to come in to some kind of reception tonight. A thousand dollars a plate? Is that what it cost? My land, child . . . A thousand dollars! Sloane and them always on to something or another. Need to spend that on some of these vacant lots we got around here. Ain't it the truth.

There were policemen and undercover-types literally everywhere. A couple of the officers would nod at Sloane or say something. Some of the others that had actually grown up in Finland Station nodded at some of the people in the demonstration line. A couple of Sloane's high school running partners grinned and nodded as they passed, now enrolled in the protection of the pretender. Some would beneath brown skin blush, and beneath the white skin, redder, they too would blush.

"Hey, Ray! What's happening?" said one dude who had become a militant cop for a minute, until Tim had him locked up for dumping garbage along with the Lloyd group. He was parked directly in front of the hotel. They'd placed him there to let the R.C. bunch see that there were defections from the revolutionary motive everywhere. Tim's aides, for instance, and many of the City Hall functionaries, were some of the biggest mouths calling for the destruction of America a few years ago. Ten thousand and up cooled them out a.s.a.p., and now some of them began to flit into the hotel. And the guests began to arrive in their finery, some of which wasn't fine at all. How come it could be that some sister making $57.50 a week, in blue jeans or cheap skirt, could be more elegant than the shadowy presences strutting their stuff with capes and jeweled bags and the rest of the garbage? A couple of these couples made the actual mistake of thinking they could walk through the park toward the set, not knowing that democracy called for it to be shut off. Some of the demonstrators lit them up at once, asking about the money and the doofus clothes that purported to be expensive.

More and more people joined the line, and it was well over three hundred when the sirens could be heard, the red eyes swooping around on top of the leading police cars. A cheer began to go up from some of the people braced around the snow fence used to cordon off the park. But this cheer was drowned out instantly by the demonstrators, who blanketed the area with heavy boos. The cheerers turned and gave the evil eye to the booers, but there weren't enough of them to matter. One provocateur walked back and forth in front of the line of demonstrators, a sick looking young Negro in a blue three-piece suit with a camera, saying, "Y'all gonna get locked up," but people blanked on him and he trailed off.

In the car directly behind the president's was Tim Goodson's, and directly behind that was Laird Conroy, President of Gratitude. Its white marble tower stood directly across the park from the hotel, and the blue neon had just turned on and beamed its steady announcement of wealth and power. Actually, Conroy almost resented the fact that Tim's car was in front of his. The governor was riding with the president, and Senator Cod rode with Tim. It was the correct protocol, but not really, if you was being for real. Actually, Conroy should have been in the first car, Jimmy.

The demonstrators could see the cars as they pulled up the street toward the hotel. The comrades with the banners had hoisted them as high as they could, in hopes that the president would see that some folks thought he was jive. But it was mostly as Goodson had said: They didn't see the president and he didn't see them.

The party got out and swept up the stairs bathed in police. If you wasn't the president, you got mashed a little bit by the zealous Secret Service and the police. It was obvious that Tim and Roger had done a good job. There was no way nothing untoward could happen.

Laird Conroy was still a trifle starchy because he trailed the president by so much while Tim and the other blacks were closer, though none of them were anywhere near because of the police ring. With Conroy were his wife, Lydia, and their children, Morgan and

Melissa. Melissa was a junior at Vassar, majoring, actually, in walking just slower than a medium gait, with head thrown slightly back and little nose reddening. Her brother was a peacenik potnik, gone straight. He and the governor's son had gotten busted a year ago for smoking bush, and that was when the governor came out with his humanitarian plea that the marijuana laws were too hard and should be reviewed. They were reviewed and the two boys got off with a stern talking-to by a judge, with Morgan being re-enrolled at Princeton, where he'd just about dropped out. He had started to go underground to classes given by the disciples of the Perfect Master Guru Rij, one of whom was a former revolutionary homosexual. The revolutionaries kept being unsympathetic to homosexuality, and that moved him more toward the Perfect Master, who understood homosexuality perfectly, like he understood everything else. But at the same time, Morgan got excited when he read about Patty Hearst. Peace was everywhere, he understood. But Patty Hearst, that excited him. They had the same experience. Trapped in the avalanche of privilege.

Tim was fine now. He shook the president's hand again. They were eating the thousand-dollar plate, and he looked over at Madeline, thinking she ought to feel better than this, sitting on the dais with the President of the United States. How many niggers can say that? Why she begrudge me a little loose booty, and I got her sitting up here with these million-dollar folks? A couple of years and a cabinet post, Jim.

"The security was fabulous, Tim, fabulous. I've heard so much about your city. The media, you know how they like to distort things. I didn't know what to expect. But you're handling things wonderfully." The president leaned over and said these things to Tim during the dinner, and he was glad that Madeline was listening and could check out how dynamite the President of the United States thought he was—the most powerful man in the world (Tim believed), what he had to say about Tim Goodson. *Shh . . . I'm the only one that could tame a tough town like this, baby.*

"Thank you, Mr. President. But we both know how the media lie, trying to sell papers." They laughed, pretending intimacy.

The dinner was being eaten up. The dessert. Politicians had risen and told jokes. A few real intimates had been upstairs at a smallish cocktail reception before the very big spenders. And they talked about the real problems. Markets. Russian contention with their business everywhere. What companies were in trouble. What Rockefeller's new house on the Pocantico, the Japanese model, was really like.

Now the president was being introduced by Governor Rose. Rose, a Democrat, nevertheless tried to sound like a member of the same team, though mentioning they were two different wings of the same American eagle. By talking about the president's personal qualities—his football years, his hardiness in the face of assassination threats, his willingness to get out and meet the American people. He was finally saying, "the President of the United States." The band went into "Hail to the Chief."

The people rose, and as they did, Morgan Conroy drew a gun out of his belt and pointed it at the president and began firing. Tim Goodson instinctively rose up as the gun was pulled. He didn't understand, but anyway, he was rising. He thought, *Why? It was a* split-second. *Why? This isn't the cabinet post!* He threw himself forward. *The cabinet post.* "What the fuck?" he was saying out loud, and he got hit by all three of the bullets that were fired. They hit him in the head—face and neck. And before young Conroy could fire again, he was inundated by waiters with .45 automatics. By that time, Goodson was dead.

The president was whizzed back to Washington. He issued a grave press release praising Goodson to the skies. An investigation was held, but it merely revealed that Morgan was spaced out and thought that this was what Patty would want. His father had to resign as President of Gratitude, but with half a million a year and stock options as his retirement. Morgan was placed in a private hospital after staying in jail for six years. Five years later, he wrote a book and began traveling around the world, snorting about $500 a week in cocaine.

Tim Goodson was buried at the largest funeral ever held in Finland Station. Black politicians came from all over the country. The vice president came, but not the president, as Finland Station was too much of a security risk. Madeline sat for hours in the house alone, thinking about what she would do. And Ray Sloane and the R.C. discussed what had happened, talking about the irony, the sick irony of it all, and went back to their job of trying to make a revolution.

1975

Norman's Date

Norman comes into the bar and tells me this one night.

Norman always had great stuff to say, about painting and people he knew and Europe. Personalities and marvelous accomplishments. Fashionable stuff, in a way. But one night he comes up with this—it knocked me out.

He's drinking. He's got one hand holding up his very expensive trench coat. He's got a Gauloise dangling outta his mouth. (That's his usual stance.) He says: I met a woman, huh, the other night. Boy! He's talking and puffing the Gauloise, his coat pushed back, a couple of guys and me listening. We got drinks. It's not even late. Nobody's drunk.

Yeh, I'd been at the Five Spot, he says. He's talking like it's real. He's earnest, ya know? I was listening to Monk. And I see this babe standing by the bar digging the music. She's listening, she smiles. She's weaving, she's got a glass. Ya know. I start watchin her.

She's great, man. Great looking. Long and slender and blond. And all dolled up, but with good taste. Even some goddamn jewelry—and I hate jewelry. But on her it looks great, really great. And she spots me after a while. I was playin' it cool, ya know? I thought maybe her ol' man was in the john and coming right back. Shit,

I didn't want no trouble. The music's great, too. That crazy Monk. And Wilbur. And that goddamn Trane is learning to play Monk's tunes, ya know?

Norman holds up his glass and gestures at us; there were maybe two others and me in our knot. He gestures for drinks all around. He's lighting another Gauloise with the stump he's got in his mouth. He shrugs acknowledgment as we hold up our glasses, saluting him. Norman was a kind of generous guy in a way, but he comes on tough. An ex-captain in the goddamn bombers during the Second World War. He's always got a scowl on his puss. People who don't know him think he's an asshole. A couple of friends of mine, even. They say Norman never invites them to his goddamn parties—the stuck-up elitist bastard. Ya know, Norman was making a little money then. Flying back and forth to Paris. Had regular shows there and a good gallery in New York. Big abstract expressionist canvasses. Big as hell, with the paint soaked in. And you could tell his Rorschach—he had his own style. You could tell a Norman *anywhere* once you'd seem them.

I got to know him through Frank. He was always jammed up with painters, especially the abstract expressionists—De Kooning, Kline, Guston, Hartigan, and even Rivers. He wasn't abstract, not on canvas anyway. I think Rivers took out his abstraction in the real world. But he would leave half a person out of his paintings. I guess as a kind of tribute to all the money the A.E.'s was making.

Cedar Bar. The early '60s, before Malcolm and hot street shit sent people flying every which way. (A buncha us to Harlem!) But we hung tough then. And bullshit—massive amounts of it got laid down in that joint.

So she looks at me, Norman's saying, right in the eye. Hey, what a look! It went right through me. My pecker started to turn over just a little bit, ya know? This babe was really good looking, no shit!

We're sipping and Norman's a good storyteller. He brings in the whole nuance of the thing. The environmental vibes, so to speak. He describes the woman. He really describes her. She sounds good, like a cross between Brigitte Bardot and Marilyn Monroe. (I think these were his references.) But not "whorish," he says, not at all whorish. Real nice!

Norman's a big square-jawed Jewish guy with a permanently sneering lower lip. It gives him character. But actually, he's a sweet guy in a lotta ways. He'd probably give you his last dime, but he ain't never gonna get to that. No, not his *last* dime, knowing Norman. He knows what's happening and being broke ain't it!

Monk's doing his wild dance. Norman demonstrates. Oh shit! I was laughing. Fuckin Norman, don't dance, please. Just get on with the goddamn story.

And the babe is getting warmer and warmer. I could feel it across the room. Warmer, right there across the room. Through the music and over the people. A not insubstantial volume—is that the term? (We spat that around. Hey, whatever.) But the babe is sending like fuckin heat-rays across the room. And I start thinking . . . I wasn't thinking shit. But the ding-dong is clearly on the move. And we're still fifteen feet apart. And Monk is squatting down and . . . Norman demonstrates again. He comes up and gestures with the glass. Sam bought another round.

When the set's over, she looks away. I say shit, what a fuckin tease. This bitch! But then the fuckin broad turns and looks me right up and down from eyehole to peehole. Yeh, she lays them baby-blue glimmers right on the tip of my pecker. We howled.

How'd you know it was the tip end? Fuckin drunk Basil always got some contentious shit to raise—he's beginning to get a little potted.

Hey, you know where somebody's looking, goddamnit. Norman pretended to be incensed. We laughed.

I said, Basil never had nobody look at his drunken ass. He's too fuckin drunk.

What? What? Basil chugalugged his brew. You wanna see the eye-prints on my ding-a-ling? (Norman made the jerk-off sign.) Everybody almost fell down.

John the bartender comes over, says, What the fuck you guys bullshittin about now? Goddamn Norman lying about something again?

John, kiss my ass, will ya, Norman said. Give us a fuckin free round and quit buttin in the customers' fuckin conversation.

So then, while she's shooting the heat-rays at my johnson, I start to return it full-up, ya know?

What'd you do, pee? (Basil again.)

Ya prick, shaddup! Let him finish. Go ahead, Norman.

It's crowded as hell in the Five Spot. Hey, where was I? I was getting it in. I'm in the Five Spot every night—Monk and Trane, man. That's bad-bad. Not just bad, but bad-bad!

Yeh, everybody said amen to that. And it was bad, bad-bad. Check the records.

So I start over, says Norman. Yeh, I start over. Not goofy like Basil.

Basil shrugged, chugalugged, and waved for another at John, who was now standing behind the bar cocking an ear. He knew the kind of good stories Norman could tell.

I start over, very cautious and cool. Like I'm moving through the crowd, like maybe I was going to the john or to somebody else's table, right?

Yeh, we encouraged.

And then when it looks like I might pass the table, I turn like slow. Norman gave the No. 1 demo of Valentino: Norman Valentino: eyes squinted sexily, shoulders pulled back, his trench coat hanging over that one arm, ever-present drink in hand. Yeh, we were clapping through our brew. Yeh, like that.

She looked up at me. Maybe she'd never taken her eyes away, I dunno. But when I turned, she caught me again from pecker to soul and back again. Whew.

We *whewed* too. John smirked, but listened even harder. Basil was grinning silently and making funny motions with his body that I decided were cheerleading stunts.

And then I'm standing there over the table, and she's whispering almost, her voice low and soft, like quiet. People all around cackling and howling like they do at intermission. Pushing back and forth. And I'm standing there with this wild-looking woman stroking me through the eyes, down clear to the balls!

Norman was outdoing himself. His metaphors were

usually sharp, but maybe this eternal story of boy meets girl (accompanied by T. Sphere Monk) was out. We were getting rapt and dumping beer down us, or whatever. No, I think I was drinking bourbon and soda.

She says, So why you standing there? There's room. I guess I kept staring. You just want to look?

Huh. I dunno if I said huh. I probably did, but she thought it was something else with the cigarette. Hi, I said, and she laughs with that uncanny, quiet, low voice.

Hi, yourself. I was wondering if you were coming over or what. I thought for a while you might be just window shopping.

I laughed and eased into the seat. I sort of held the glass up like a little toast as I sat, and she did the same.

Whatcha drinking? It's always my first statement to any broad, no matter how she looks. She's drinking that goddamn Dubonnet on the rocks. I shoulda . . .

What? Basil snapped out of his slow drunken grin. Dubonnet, for Christ's sake! Who the hell drinks that?

Shaddup, drunk, will ya? I think it was White propped against the bar, at least as drunk as Basil, kibitzing. I wanna hear the goddamn story.

OK, OK. Basil started to order another round, but John was already drawing it. So what happened next, Norman? Goddamnit, this is getting good. And Basil begins to chugalug again.

Yeh, we start talking, ya know? I tell her about me. She said she'd seen some of my work at Castelli's. She tells me she was even at an opening of mine.

Yay, a fuckin art lover! Basil was smirking and White was frowning at him an unserious frown.

She tells me she used to paint when she first came

to the Village, but got bored. She worked at an ad agency. She was a model. She even went out to Hollywood.

Yay, Hollywood! White cheered.

Shaddup, drunken bastard, Basil jeered unseriously.

So what's she do then? I wanted to keep the story moving. Stories turn me on, especially from guys like Norman, because you keep waiting for some slip-up so you can tell it's bullshit, or else it's real and you pick up some info.

She says she's thinking about it. She says she saved up some money so she's between careers. She even wanted to play the goddamn violin—took lessons and everything. But nothing.

Anyway, we're getting cozy—Monk comes back out. She keeps on with the Dubonnet and I'm sloshing down bourbon and waters like they're gonna ration the shit the next day. She's purring at me. Asking me about art. Asking me about my life.

She tells me she never married. That she lived with a few guys a couple times, but nothing serious. She's twenty-seven—just my age category. (Norman was thirty-seven then.) And man, once I got close to her, she looked even better. Smooth ivory skin. Pale lips. These blue-gray peepers that seemed like they wanted to change colors. And then Norman chugalugs. And a set of fuckin—he makes a cupping motion—breasts.

Basil and White turned and squinted at Norman at the same time. I was laughing, so it made a little sound of air rushing out between my teeth. We almost said at the same time, *Breasts?*

Wow, after the air, I let out what we all had got

simultaneously. Hey, Norman, I've never heard you say "breasts" before. I thought them things upon the ladies' chests was boobs. Or boobies. Ain't that what he calls them?

Right.

Yep.

White and Basil chimed in.

Norman with a goddamn woman with some breasts is hard to take. It was White's most coherent statement of the evening.

There were breasts, lads. And he got another setup from John. John was shaking his head back and forth. Come on, Norman. Don't slow down now. Let's hear about the goddamn breasts, for Christ's sake!

By the end of Monk's set, we were both mellow. We already got the next day planned out. Lunch, a trip to my gallery, a show. More Monk and Trane the next night. Then she says, I think it's time to head in. If we get too drunk we'll only sleep.

It was the desired turning point of the story. All the circle of the narrated-to got closer, and armed with the last free drink, we licked our lips and waited for the next installment. Even Domenick, who was half-listening and half-trying to ignore Norman 'cause he didn't like him, cocked a blatant ear and dragged his eyes off a passing lady-painter's ass.

Yeh, she says that. I hadn't even asked to go to her place. But she just pops out with it—bam! Sleep, hell, hold on. I'm not in a sleepin' mood. Alcohol don't put me to sleep. It just makes me mean. And she laughed that low laugh and her eyes seemed to change colors. Like, like . . .

Like what? I was pressing.

No, let me finish.

Go ahead!

I like that in men, she says. Mean and very physical.

Wow, Basil said. Wow. She said very physical, huh? You shoulda called White.

Shaddup, drunk. Go on, Norman.

You're coming home with me, right? she says.

Hey, you ain't even told us the woman's name, I put in. It just occurred to me. Maybe this was the slip-up, I thought.

He don't wanna tell us her name because he wants to keep a good thing secret, Domenick spoke for the first time, a little ironically and a trifle sour.

Shaddup, Domenick, Basil grinned. You didn't tap nobody on the shoulder when that last fat ass floated by, either. Domenick was cooled out.

Monica. Monica Hess, Norman said straightforwardly.

Oh, a German babe. I came on with some academic shit.

Yeh, I guess, but she didn't press it. She said she'd grown up in a small town in the Midwest—in Ohio, actually. In fact, she comes from a town called Hess, Ohio, named after her fuckin grandfather.

Wow, we howled. That this bastard scored was the general sentiment. A fuckin painter and a rich bitch.

A rich sexy . . .

Beautiful.

Yeh.

Bitch.

Smoke would get in Norman's eyes and he'd squint.

And you wouldn't really know sometimes what kind of expression was on his face.

She told me a lot about herself, her childhood. All the different careers. She said she couldn't find a man to satisfy her, either.

Wow, a general wow, came from us. And the anticipation hooked up together like a rope.

To satisfy her? White hunched Basil so sharply that Basil *ugghed* in drunken pantomime like it hurt. It did, but he was too drunk to care.

So you naturally volunteered for that gig, I chuckled.

Yeh. Norman was grinning now, a strange light in his eyes. Yeh, I volunteered alright. On the goddamn spot. My pecker was starting to rise like the fuckin flag on the 4th of July! So we get to her place, ya know? She lives on 4th Avenue.

Hey, you know they're going to call that Park Avenue South in a little while?

Fuck them, White spat. It's 4th Avenue, not no fuckin Park Avenue South!

Fuckin a tweety! Basil wet us with his affirmation.

Come on with the story, Norman. It was Domenick, maybe thinking Norman's ending would be so weak it would give the whole thing up as bullshit. Norman never even looked at him. He rasped at John through the open end of his lips. Buy the loud guy a drink on me.

Where on 4th Ave.?

You know the building that looks like a convent or tourist attraction in an old European village?

Yeh.

By the bookstore, across from the post office.

Yeh. Hey, that's a pretty heavy looking building. What's the goddamn rent in there?

She says she pays 450 a month.

What? (And this was the early '60s when that was even further out than it is today.)

Four-fifty?

Jeez, what's in the goddamn place?

Hey, it's worth it. The inside of the joint is no quaint shit. It's super modern. (Norman used the French pronunciation so the whole effect was got.) And get this, there's a goddamn doorman inside. But we go around to a back entrance on Broadway she's got a key for. Go to an elevator, and get this—the elevator only stops at her floor.

Everybody was now sufficiently impressed. On the real side.

I pressed. You mean everybody in that joint got their own elevators?

I dunno. She says she dunno either. But she has.

Wow.

So we slide right in and up. The elevator door opens right into her apartment.

Yeh?

And it's laid out gorgeous. Rugs everywhere. Not the wall-to-wall, but different Indian and Persian rugs. Oriental rugs in different parts of a hardwood floor. She's got modern furniture in some rooms, old antiques in others. Glass and leather and plastic shit some places. Wood and easy-chairs other places. The living room is modern. She's got paintings everywhere.

Any of yours?

Yeh, yeh. She had a big orange painting that Castelli

sold last year. It's called *Orange Laughter*. But she had a Kline, a Guston, a big De Kooning woman. A fuckin Larry Rivers naked woman.

Like the one he did of Frank with the dangling pecker?

No—it was more modest. Norman was being ironic. Hey, she had a Frankenthaler. A goddamn Rauschenberg. A Jasper Johns.

What the hell is this woman, a goddamn art buyer? Basil.

She's just got money, fool. White.

Art buyers got money.

I said, She told you she *saved* money? Ho ho ho!

No, she's loaded. It's maybe an eight-room apartment. A couple bedrooms, guest room, full kitchen. Books. Records. Big Fisher components. Speakers in all the rooms. She pushed a button and there's a goddamn Morty Feldman piano concerto on.

Fat-ass Morty!

So what happens, man? Shaddup, you guys!

We listen to Morty. We listen to Earl Brown. John Tudor and John Cage. Monk. We drink. We talk. The view is great—great! We lay in front of her goddamn fireplace. She even played some Basie and we danced. We talked and talked. And then we got undressed on the floor. What a body!

Everybody was pushed forward now, heads thrust at Norman like they could see the big pretty breasts and round peachlike behind. The long blond hair draped around her when she let it down, cushioning her head and neck and back, and the downstairs hair yellow too, and the odor coming out of her. Norman almost sung about her like some goose-pimpling eau de cologne called Fuck Me Now Immediately Daddy Do Not Dally Any Further!

So we did it first on the floor. She undressed like her clothes were burning her. But it was sexy, mate, I tell you. And there she was. And in a few seconds—

There were you, I shot in.

Yeh.

Laughter.

And what is there to say about big thighs pulling open of their own accord? And eyes hot as a weird blue stove?

Wow.

A couple hours later, we go again. She's quieter now, but clings real tight. She even dug her nails in my back just a little when the whistle blew.

Yeh, yeh, yeh! We whistled and beat on the chairs.

Yeh, Norman. Tell it. White wobbled.

And then just before we go to sleep—it's about 2 now—she tells me a little saying her mother told her. It went: No matter how much you might get hurt, there's love that can heal you.

Was it good, Norman? Basil smirked.

It was very, very good. Exquisite body. And she knew what she was doing. She knew all the right spots.

No matter how much you might hurt, I repeated, there's love that can heal you.

Yeh, I felt good. Hey, it was heavenly. Heavenly. And then she sang a little song. Some kind of folk tune. Maybe it was European, I dunno. I thought it was Mother Goose or something. No words, just humming and a kind of refrain she repeated.

Hey, man, that sounds great. White had stood up

straight to speak. Getting as sober as he could for the official congratulations.

Heavy stuff, young Norman, I added.

Hooray for Norman! Basil sputtered. Not only do people buy his paintings, but he gets to fuck beautiful girls that sing, for Christ's sake! This tickled Domenick.

But then Norman looked at us with another thing in his face and voice. Yeh, it was good. I thought it was beautiful, the fire and all. I even picked her up and carried her and laid her in the big bed.

Hey, that's a line from Frank Yerby, I kibitzed him, admiringly so. Frank Yerby.

Yeh. Norman puffed and puffed on the cigarette now. And John had a big smile, pulling his head up and down slowly, affirming the reality of the tale.

But then I went to the window, finished another bourbon and smoked a Gauloise, and looked down at 4th Avenue.

It was that cool, huh?

Yeh. And after that, I went and lay down beside her. In the little night light, I could still see how beautiful she was, and I thought, Shit, it's my fuckin lucky period. Goddamn. So I lay out. I was painting pretty good. Another show in a couple months. A couple bucks in my pocket. And this fantastic sweet thing next to me in the half-dark.

Wow.

Norman got another drink and pulled himself straight.

Wow.

Yeh, wow, he said, his eyes clouding over like a windshield without a defroster on a suddenly frosty day. And then, about an hour or so later, I guess—I was sleeping—and I dunno, I just felt . . . Something just got in me. Something woke me up.

Uh-huh.

And I open my eyes, raise up a little in bed. My eyes had to get used to the half-dark. But I notice too that Monica is also raised up in bed. Full up. My eyes focus and I can suddenly see her. She's sitting there, man, straight up in bed . . . And she's got a pair of scissors held up in the air! And now she can see that I see her, and our eyes meet.

What? It came from all of us at once, and the word just hung a second in the whistling smoke, half-crumpled and half-floated to the floor.

But I could tell—I could see—that Norman wasn't lying. He wasn't. And now he was repeating the last part again, so it could really penetrate.

Yeh, she was sitting there in the dark with a pair of fuckin scissors.

Why? Basil finally asked, almost sober now.

We looked at each other and at Norman.

Norman coughed from the smoke in his face, the cigarette still dangling. His eyes playing over us, convincing us without the least opposition. What you mean, *Why?* he was saying. How the fuck would I know? I sure as hell wasn't staying around to find out.

We all finally let it go, the caged-up air—the surrogate terror in it, and even an inch of curious delight. Norman's eyes glowed a little and he grinned the grin of the escaped hunter.

A cold glaze replaced his living eyes, and the ice of death came into his face. The cigarette should have dropped, but it was stuck to his bottom lip, even with his mouth hung open.

What's happening? I, the rest of us, looked at Norman, then turned to look over our shoulders. There was a blond woman now standing just inside the bar's entrance.

She began to walk toward us. I thought, Hey, now Norman's slip-up is coming right straight out with the lying shit. But Norman looked ashen. I didn't think a mere lie could do that. We were all starting to grin. I guess it had also occurred to the others too that what Norman had told us was a really well-told lie. And now, here was the chick in person to uncover the lie.

But before our smiles could tumble into place and replace our quizzical stares, Norman's ashen silence transmitted a howl of deep fear to us all. Not light-weight bullshit. So when we looked at the woman striding straight toward us, unnoticed by the rest of the raucous barflies, what we saw made us all believers. Believers forever in all the unknown spaces of terror, the blankness between the stars.

The bitch still had a pair of scissors in her hand. And as she came toward us, she held them up and waved them slowly back and forth, like a wand. But they were covered, even dripping, with very fresh blood.

1981–82
(Originally published in Playboy, *July 1983)*

From War Stories

Back before the jogging thing got to be a "craze," during the late '60s or so, I used to go out every couple of days and run around the half-mile track at Wake-wake Park. In those days, and to my mind, the body was what the mind was, and so I was out all the time, flying around the track. Also, I'd take off at least once a week and go zooming around the lake itself, about three miles or so. It brought back my high school cross country days. The wind in your face, talking to yourself, and thinking great, out of breath, slightly agonized thoughts.

The funny part of this regimen was that at the time I weighed about 120 pounds, soaked in lead allegory. I ate no meat—the result of a bout with the Air Force in which I was served bleeding chicken on Sunday afternoons. From then on, I used to trade my chicken, a weekly affair, for salad or dessert or just straight-out gave it away. It carried over into real life, life after the error farce, so that now even in my thirtieth year, I still shudderingly refrained from eating meat.

So early mornings I'd dash around Wake-wake, named after Indians who'd been bested in a land deal. Its name seemed to be both a command and a solemn gathering.

I was also a member of a political action committee

in Noah at the time. Noah, New Jersey, population 300,000, mostly colored. Quite a few Negroes, a few black people, plus significant numbers of Italians, Puerto Ricans, and Portuguese. I'm telling you this not only to help accurately portray my general state of mind, but to tell you that at least one day a week, usually Saturday, a whole bunch of us in the PAC would be running, staying in shape. A few of us believed that democracy for the assorted groups of colored, Negroes, and blacks could be won by refraining from eating meat and jogging, plus karate. An even smaller group of us thought that it might take more than that—maybe a little Malcolm, a little Che, a little Mao, some Ron Karenga, Carmichael, and pinches of some other folk, living and dead. Hey, there was even a smaller group that didn't care at all. And you know, I later found out that there was a group larger than all of the above who figured it would take even more than that.

At any rate, running through the park, not during the Saturday mass sessions but alone, with the leaves' shadows visibly crossing your hands and arms; the sun streaming through the green overgrowth to get to you; the air thin and delicious, being sucked in desperately as you came up that series of dead man's hills before the long downhill straightaway that brought you in past the school stadium and to the finish—that was something else. You felt strong and somehow motivated. You had to succeed because you were succeeding already. Running free, so to speak.

The Saturday sessions were regulated mass affairs. We might run—not might, *did* run—around the same lake. And that was great: catching up to people, being passed by the jocks and a few sworn killers who had to win to prove their absolute sincerity to the cause of the people. The camaraderie and exchanged strength of that was alone worth the whole experience. Afterwards, we might play ringaleerio or touch-football or basketball or baseball. It was full-out physicality we wanted on those Saturdays. The women went out together while we were doing this—a group of young men, mostly single, but many like myself were married, already with children, and some growing sense of ourselves.

The pattern was the weekly mass outings for the collective swelling and growing we were trying to do. Plus, I'd go out a few times a week by myself, because I liked to run. I'd run two and a half for the cross country team in high school and college. Actually, it was a form of meditation, a way for me to get into myself, to let my mind go out and bring back whatever it could. A light wind against my face.

That could be all in passing. I mean, I could relate that running to the later fad or craze and we could speculate as to how that came about. I guess that period of the late '60s and early '70s was a period of people pushing themselves, of ideals, of holding oneself up to measure against any number of arbitrary goals or models, convincing oneself, with small difficulty, that the world was the way we wanted it to be. That no matter how horrible it appeared, it was the way we wanted it to be, and we could change it with the assorted words and images we tried to retain inside our otherwise very healthy heads. That itself would be an interesting conversation—limited, but still interesting.

But this is not it. This is about something else, perhaps something much simpler.

During this period of running, there was a lot going on. I can't get into all of that here—it'd scare some people and bore others. But let's say that while I was running—at the moment of, but also when I went away from Wake-wake, which was most of the time—there was a whole lot going on in Noah. A whole lot going on around the country and throughout the world. You remember the '60s, don't you? Well at any rate, you can read about it and whatnot.

Our political action committee was formed to elect black politicians to office. That's what it really was for. Some of us had more grandiose ideas, either vaguer or more specific, but if there was a consensus, it could be focused on that. We wanted to elect black politicians to office because there weren't any in Noah. Well, there was one guy, sort of the Jackie Robinson of black politicians. John Walker was his real name. Some of us called him Johnnie Walker Black, after the Scotch. Plus, he'd always have a few glasses of that running around in his system somewhere. He was a good guy—he had been a good guy. When I was a kid, he was a real hero. The first black councilman and whatnot. He knew my parents, and everybody in those days supported him. But he'd stayed around too long. He'd gotten to be too well known for his real self, or the self that had come to be seen by everybody. He'd had a couple of unsuccessful marriages, one to a friend of my mother's who was a nurse and didn't want to let go of her job, even back then in the early '50s. They'd split. He'd started to become a noticeable drinker and an even more noticeable drunk. Sometimes (most times), he'd inhabit a kind of twilight zone between the living and the dead, his eyes rolling open every so often, his dry cracked lips poking open momentarily to suck up some trifling air, and then he'd roll over and go deep off into a primordial ancient pygmy sleep. This would be while sitting in his First Negro Councilman Chair, under a portrait of him as the First Negro Councilman, in front of everybody—white folks too.

Plus, blacks or Negroes or colored were a majority (all of the aforementioned, together) in Noah. The gray industrial countercharm of Noah, which I'd grown up in, had by the '60s lost most of its hold on anybody who had options, mainly the socially mobile, mostly white middle class, and they'd gotten in the wind. Any other colors of middle class had got in the wind too, mostly, though it must be clear that there were some of us still around pouting that now that we were here almost by ourselves, we still didn't have any power or control over anything. (I remember shouting at Mr. French, the curator of the museum, that while I like the internationally famous Tibetan collection—I'd grown up on it, snaking around those masks and vases, still in elementary school, trying to sniff out my own essence—that, damn! couldn't there be something that more resembled myself? The Hudson River School paintings were great—I'd grown up on them too—but damn, what about a picture of Headlight, Bubbles, Roggie, Kenny, and me coming down Belmont Avenue, sharp as African mythology, heading to the Graham Auditorium for the Sunday night "Canteen"? Like where was that, my man?)

The tremors of those years? The rush of trying to be resolved frustrations. The hungers and thirsts. One stretch, I actually thought I was carrying the slave ship around in my head. I kept hearing the drums and screams, the savage slash of the whips. And the ship was nearing the shore, and it was the middle of winter. I kept peering out of a hole in the ship, just about the waterline, I guess, and saw this icy, snowy land draw near. Johnnie Walker Black seemed to be slumped against Plymouth Rock with a red cap on his head, grinning but drunk as a mojo.

But this is not a tale of frustration, per se. This is perception and rationale. We did what we set out to do, our political action committee. Yessiree! We pulled a convention together and selected candidates and actually elected most of them. No shit! We organized and educated and worked our asses off. Our committee got larger and larger as people began to understand clearly what we were about, without being put off by the media.

And the committee was right in the middle of it too. We had a hand in screening candidates, setting up the entire convention, putting out the publicity, mobilizing people to show up, and then the follow-through for the election.

We brought in all kinds of celebrities and leaders from all over the country—Bill Cosby, Dustin Hoffman, James Brown. Raised money for the candidates that came out of the convention, and goddamnit, got them elected too. Not all of them, but out of the seven we ran, four got elected, even a goddamn mayor! Yeh, it was fantastic. You don't remember that? It was in all the papers, across the country. It was like the first black mayor of a major northeastern city! Yeh, that's right. Right!

A great night that was too. People came out in the streets and danced up and down, holding hands and laughing. There was a band on top of a bus, sitting in the middle of Broad Street, and black folks and Puerto Ricans and our allies flowed downtown from all parts of the city to have the great moment in Robert Treat Hall (named after the gentleman who'd actually pulled off the Indian deal). That was the height of something. The pinnacle, the goal, whatever. A thousand times heavier than making that last dead man hill and trudging but floating at the same time toward the stadium finish. A thousand-thousand times. Hey, for a minute it seemed like I was brothers with all the people I could see. Like maybe even all the life and color that was inside me, that I carry (and you carry too), could come on out, just like how we all flowed together toward Robert Treat. That what was inside me could flow on out and mingle with all the other insides that could flow out. Because, I don't know, it was amidst all the screaming and jumping up and down, absolutely safe to reveal your feelings. You know?

I feel like laughing now. No, I *am* laughing. HAHA-HAHAHAHAHAHAHAHAHAHAHAHAHAHAHAHAHA! No, it's nothing. I just thought of something. Not thought of something. The park, the running. We've gotten so far away from that, it seems. Wake-wake Park. Gee, I think of old Henry Deel, who just died. He was almost the mayor, but we thought . . . There was some kind of minor scandal or something. I don't even remember. And "Sweets" Towne, that old Democratic hustler, was always in it. He even threatened me specifically one night for talking bad about Johnnie Walker Black and trying to rip off his own meal ticket. But he was alright too, actually. Boy, did we talk bad to and about white folks in those days. I saw this one dopey woman recently that we put out of the theatre. She was trying to pass then as a Russian Indian. A sister told her she had to leave the Russian outside. I saw her, that same woman, walking down the street with a guy who actually looked like a Russian Indian, just a couple of days ago.

The park? The running, really. I miss that. Doesn't time fly? No, I don't run too much—I switched from Wake-wake awhile ago. Started running from my house, about four long blocks, to get the newspapers, then I even stopped that. I dunno. The guy we elected, Kent Winston. Yeh, you know him? Yeh, now you got it. Well, he never came out to the park too much until after he got elected. Then he'd come out often. One time, I remember seeing him running before the election and I zoomed past him, not maliciously, but he was running much slower than my pace. He said something to me as I passed, like "cross country." He'd grown up in Noah too, and he knew why I could set such a hot pace. It was funny.

But a couple of months after the election, I'm running around the lake. I'm still not up to the dead man's hills, but I hear a horn honking like it's right out on the road. And guess what, there's Winston, running the opposite way. I mean, he's running so the hills are reversed, running downhill most of it instead of that killer uphill climb the hills represent if you're running those three miles the regular way.

Winton's running the wrong way, but it's a little different. Just behind him was this big black Lincoln and inside are two cops—two plainclothes Negroes, Winston's bodyguards. They're all "jogging"— Winston, the two cops, and the Lincoln. I had to step off the side of the path and run in place while Winston waved and passed. I think I ran in place for a few seconds, think I just stopped. Flat out.

But I don't think that's why I stopped going to Wake-wake to run. Maybe, but I don't think so. What stopped me from running there, early in the morning by myself, was when those two Muslim brothers got killed, supposedly as payback for knocking off this minister of the Muslim temple in Noah. There were always rumors about that temple. It was even said that Malcolm X's killers had come out of there. And there had also always been rumors about the various "renegade" Muslims who sold drugs and ran the numbers, who'd turn the money in at the Noah temple.

Later, there'd been some breakaway movement. I think it was called Brothers of the New Age. Some folks said it all had to do with the pushers and gamblers not wanting to turn the money over anymore, so that a sharp conflict developed inside the temple. One afternoon, somebody'd blown the Imam of the Noah temple to kingdom come. He was shot up close, as he'd come out of his house on the way to the temple.

Of course, the whole Muslim community was in an uproar and there were Muslim brothers supposedly searching Noah furiously for the assassins. Apparently they found them too, or at least some dudes who'd fit the description. Early one morning, the two guys' *heads* were found by the lake, just off the running path. Yeh, the heads of the twin brothers were left there, blood still drying at the severed necks, right down by the lake. I think that's what killed it for me. I never went jogging there again.

August 15–September 5, 1982
Correction Facility, New York City

Mondongo

Y ou never go anywhere, Ray. Believe me, I know where you go. And you don't go anywhere. Not around here, I mean, where everybody can see." Irv Laffawiss pushed his "cunt cap" back on his head so he looked like the posters of the sloppy airmen in the slides shown at Character Guidance lessons on Saturdays. He should have had a red X painted across him to resemble the classic well-advertised "Sad Sack" of U.S. military tradition. And it was the U.S. military, the Air Force, in which he and his good friend, Ray Johns, were now entrapped.

Johns was reading, it looked like. But he had on dark glasses and the lights in the room were low, so how he was accomplishing this reading was vague. But Laffy knew from repeated encounters not to get involved in any conversation with Ray about how it was he could read in the near-dark with dark sunglasses.

To the inquiry about "not going anywhere," Ray Johns merely peeped up over the book and stared at Laffy, "Hey, man. Why I got to go off the base? I ain't lost nothin' out there."

"You're too weird, Johns." Laffawiss sounded mildly annoyed. "Don't you believe in R&R?"

Ray Johns turned over on the bed where he was half-sprawled. He knew Laffy was going on with the conversation, so he wanted to see how he looked when he said this shit. "R&R? Shit, man. I wanna go home. Naw, I wanna go to fuckin Greenwich Village. R&R?"

"Don't you believe in girls, then?" Laffy was pressing it. He was leaning now against one of the walls, smoking a bent cigarette and flicking the ashes like Groucho Marx. Groucho was Laffy's alter ego. He enraged the non-coms and officers by coming into their office or his own room when there might be an inspection or something, bent at the waist, holding his cigarette like Groucho's cigar and striding in crazy-looking, rolling his eyes like a roulette wheel.

"Yeh, Laffawiss, I believe in girls. Why, you got any?"

Laffy pointed over his shoulder and imitated Groucho: "They went that-a-way!" Pointing in the general direction of the town—in this case, Aguadilla, a nasty little dot at the tip of Puerto Rico's shore. Laffawiss and Johns, together with 5,000 other airmen, were stationed just outside Aguadilla at the SAC base, Ramey. They, along with the others, commanded by a thirty-eight-year-old nutty general who wanted to clean up venereal disease, were busy with the task of keeping the free world free and intimidating any sons-of-bitches who wanted to maybe make wise remarks, or rape freckle-faced girls, or live too close, or talk in funny languages, or smell or look funny, or communize the country—any of that stuff. They were doing this by means of the B-36 bomber. Laffawiss was a radio operator without a crew, and Johns a weather-gunner in the worst crew on the base.

Every weekend and maybe more, Laffawiss would

"roar into town," as the airmen described, get drunk, pay for some pussy, then stagger back to the base with a head as big as a propeller. Johns and Laffawiss were pretty good friends, Johns from a large town in Jersey close to Manhattan and Laffawiss from the Lower East Side. Not the Lower East Side of boutiques and poetry readings, but the old East Side of Mike Gold's heroes and heroines of herrings, kosher pickles, pushcarts, and poverty.

Johns was a college boy, a dropout from a black school trying to find himself. Mostly by reading everything that would sit still long enough to be read, including gruesome adventures like reading the whole of the *Times* best-seller list in a month. The complete works of Marcel Proust, James Joyce, Ernest Hemingway, &c. Hours and hours of guard duty pulled by Johns had turned reading from an informative pastime to a physical and psychological addiction. He got so he could read anything—no, not could, had to. The sight of words on paper inflamed him, turned him on in a way nothing else could. Sometimes when he slept uneasily under the Puerto Rican moon, he dreamed of reading, pages flowing effortlessly through his sleep.

His barracks room, which he shared with a giant country boy from Long Island (now, thank god, on leave), had, despite the pressures of would-be military standard operating procedures, begun to take on the look of a second-hand bookstore.

Every week, Johns had to hear something from one of the non-coms about the room and its unmilitary look. You were only supposed to have "pictures of loved ones," and as many books as the dresser top would allow to sit "in a military manner." But then he had to hear about the weak little fuzz he had sprouting out the edge of his chin, which the "war cats" insisted was a beard. Or the "boot salute," which many of the black troops threw in lieu of the war one, viz, this was where the head was bent down to meet the reluctant right hand, producing a "blood salute." Especially them Southern white officers didn't dig this. Johns once had to stand and salute about forty times in the hot sun, "until he got it right." And he did, "by god," as the game started to tire him and the hot sun had got all in the young blond lieutenant's uniform, wetting him to the skin.

Between Laffawiss, the scrawny humpbacked Groucho "Jew bastard," as some of the quainter Southern boys called him, and Johns, "a fuckin nigger snob," many incorrect and backward dudes did they light up with their wild antics. Both were young men sufficiently turned around by their younger lives and what they were learning now in "this war shit" (although it was peacetime, between the Korean and Vietnam Wars). Both had the beginning of the stiff self-identification of themselves as intellectuals, whatever that meant to them. And it didn't mean too much, except both liked to read, both were mostly quiet and inner-directed, and they both hated most of the assholes that passed for non-coms and officers in the error farce, plus a whole lot of them "farmer mother-fuckers" who would batter at their sanity with endless hours of "In the Jailhouse Now," which was the top country-and-western hit of the period. Either that or Patti Page singing, "We'll Be Together Again."

They were dragged away from civilian life by their own confusion, Johns being tossed out of school for making his studies secondary to his social education, and Laffawiss because he didn't realize (either) that school did have some merit—even though you couldn't learn a hell of a lot around those people. But shit, Laffy found out he was learning a hell of a lot less around Curtis LeMay's (SAC C.O.) relatives and friends.

Both hung around a large group of full, semi, and closeted intellectuals, all now lamenting their being trapped and martyred in the Air Force, when, hell, all had joined voluntarily. They figured they were escaping the "malaise" of post-adolescence, but now they were in the real fucking malaise with not much white bread either.

A few nights a week, Johns worked as the evening librarian; and the old career special-services librarian, seeing Ray was a book nut, let him have run of the place, including being in charge of ordering books and records. So a few nights a week, Ray, Laffy, and the rest of the crowd would ease into the library, draw the blinds, break out the cheap rum and vodka, and play music most of the night—in both luxury and captivity at the same time.

But Johns almost never left the base. Only sometimes by himself would he catch the *gua gua* and end up in San Juan, preferably *viejo* San Juan, to wander around the wild and pretty streets, lamenting his fate. And Laffawiss, though not altogether gregarious, still occasionally wanted his on-base walking buddy to dare the wilds of the island with him. Shit, at least Aguadilla.

But Ray, most times, just rolled over and flipped a page, or maybe he'd just turn up the box and check what Beethoven or Bird might have to say. Or maybe just wonder what Monk was thinking behind those weird blue glasses.

"Johns, are you masturbating?" Laffy could get rude like that. Matter of fact, that was his standard tone.

"Why, you bottling jerk-off come?" Neither laughed, though they were amused.

"Naw, I just wanna find out how come you don't have a go into town and release your tension." Laffy made a lurid leer with the Groucho face on, swiveling his hips.

"Why, you think my tension needs to be released? Shit, my tension can do anything it fuckin want to. Can't you, tension?" He looked down at his fly, but there was no immediate answer.

Laffy snickered at this, picking up a water glass as if it was a microscope. "Aha, now we are entering the area of microbiology," he said, as he squinted in the same area Ray Johns made believe he was talking to. A perfect comedy team, though a trifle avant garde and abstruse for some of their buddies and anti-buddies.

Now they stalked the streets of Aguadilla, in which thousands of restless, sex-starved, largely ignorant troops were released during the evening. And there were always incidents, always unpleasantness (which included drunkenness, fighting, and sometimes cutting and shooting). And, of course, most of the people of Aguadilla just tried the best they could to do the shit they had to do to survive. But imagine being just outside the gate, and being invaded each evening by about 5,000 screaming crazed American airmen. Jeez, what about releasing them, this evening, into Darien? What about Scarsdale or Palo Alto or Basking Ridge? Yeh, yeh. I'd like to film that, boy. Or hire somebody to film that shit. Like a military-suburban *Animal House*, if you catch my sniff.

This Friday evening it was already a little late, as it had taken Laffy an hour or so to convince Ray Johns to come on in and play cowboy. Assorted airmen of all shapes, sizes, and colors were staggering, dragging, heaving, and spinning past them, the number increasing each half-hour or so as that Friday wound its way out. Most of the troops were in little groups with their buddies, some stumbled alone, and the lucky ones were already with some local women.

Laffawiss swiveled his head around on his neck, leering his Groucho leer. "That's one, Johns. That's one. A woman, ya see?"

"Yeh, I see. Very interesting."

"There's another one. You see, they got different features and all."

"Very interesting. So what happens now? My tension ain't been released. Not a bit. Is this all you have to do, twist your head off at the neck? Somehow, I thought it was going to be more complicated than this."

"Wow, first you don't even wanna leave the base and stop your meat-pulling, now you wanna turn into the original flesh fiend."

"Yeh, yeh." Johns whooped a little weakly, in celebration of some of those "farmer motherfuckers" who could be heard, even now, up and down the street whooping cowboy and confederate war cries.

Walking in the direction the way they were headed brought them face to face with *The American*, the first of the near-base bars for mainly white soldiers. Harry Truman had already desegregated the Armed Forces alright, but just as in the rest of American life, the separation still existed. So there were white bars and colored bars and a few fairly mixed. But most, even there in Puerto Rico, were either one or the other.

The American was notorious, anyway. Black and white soldiers had frequently locked asses inside its doors. And a few times, the place had been closed with *Off-Limits* signs put up. Laffy got to the door first and pushed it open, peering in.

"Why you come to this joint, Laffawiss? You gotta meet some old Klan buddies in there? Jeez, Laffy, let's not get into no abstract shit."

Laffawiss looked over his shoulder. "Hey, we're stalking our prey, man. I thought you were trying to release your tension."

"In *The American*? Ain't nothing in there but farmhouse motherfuckers. And they got all them bitches in there sick as them." Johns meant that the more backward of the white soldiers would try as quickly as possible to infect the local women with their own anti-black views. First, because they themselves had been long-shaped by the sickness of racism, but also, more practically, they were trying to protect their choice pieces of *chocha* from getting "pulled" by the aggressive black troops. Hence, fights in and around *The American* and a lot of other places, in this "neutral zone" outside the U.S. mainland, where the "bitch pulling" competition was conducted by a slightly different set of rules.

"I ain't goin in that lousy joint." Johns stepped back from the doorway as two obvious "farmer cats" stumbled by, tossing him a death look. They pushed past Laffawiss, who was still peeping in the door, seeing what he could see and talking to Ray over his shoulder.

"Hey, they're all dogs in here anyway." Then, in response to being slightly shoved by the drunken duo, Laffy added, "Creeps, you'll probably die with clap of the mouth."

"Laffawiss, let's go. I ain't in no goddamn boxing mood, man. You don't want to release tension—you want to build the shit up." Johns turned now as if he was going to leave Laffawiss in front of the bar.

"Hey, Ray—shit! Shit, Ray. Look who's in this joint." The sight of *whoever* was cracking Laffy up. "Hey, look. Come on, it'll do you good. Come on, look!"

Reluctantly, Johns crept up toward the pushed-open bar door and peered in. There were two white airmen in uniform, or mostly in uniform, their "cunt caps" or other class-A visorless caps sliding all the way to the back of their heads. Or else there were those in what was supposed to be "civilian clothes," which included "Hawaiian"-inspired obscenities as shirts, loud trousers, jeans, some pants high-styled with contrasting "pistol pockets" and seams. Bottles, mostly beer, being raised. Loud profane talking and shouting, confederate whoops, and spaced appropriately throughout the joint, on the stools and at the tables, different sizes, shapes, and colors of Puerto Rican women—some prostitutes, some not. The soldiers in the bar didn't care too much one way or the other, as long as they got over. (If they could still get it up after falling down and throwing up on each other.)

But Laffawiss was pointing now, almost frantically, at a fat, stoop-shouldered, red-faced white Airman Second with his "cunt cap" cocked way over on the side of his head. But not far over enough to hide the screaming red knife scar dug into a white valley down his cheek. Laffawiss could not contain himself. He was laughing out loud and jiggling from one foot to the other.

"What?" Ray Johns stared into the now fully lit bar. "Oh, it's that goddamn farmer that Grego cut. Wowee, first time I seen that sucker since Jack the Ripper got his ass."

Grego was a Mexican-American airman who hung with Laffy and Ray and the others in their little light-weight intellectual gang. Grego was blond and you couldn't tell he was Chicano until he opened his mouth. Or unless you spotted the tiny cross tattooed between his thumb and forefinger, which marked him *pachuco* and a member of one of the hard-ass Chicano youth gangs that littered the Southwest and L.A.

The fat farmer had made the mistake of saying something about "spics," and lickity-split, before you knew it, light caught for an instant in a blue blade passing through the air on the way to slash the man's puss, and unless he got plastic surgery, it remains so slashed until this moment.

Johns now howled too, a little cooler. But at least Laffy hadn't started pointing at the dude and hollering, *Cut that motherfucker too short to shit!*

The farm boy was apparently sitting with friends, and Laffy and Ray were the only ones from their own group, so after another second or two of acid kibitzing, including, "You should thank Grego, motherfucker, that scar at least makes your face interesting. Shit!" there was an abrupt about-face by the two laughers, as First Sergeant Barfell called out at our two heroes, and they got in the wind.

They cut around the corner and crossed a vacant lot, and presto, they were standing close by the Estrella Negra. Actually, it was simply Estrella, "Star"—The Star Bar. (The Negra had been added by both the black and white troops.) It was the big hangout for the blacks and the Latins and the white soldiers that swung with the Bloods.

White (who was not), Perkins (who was), and Yodo (who was from outer space) were sitting and standing at the bar, arguing whether Fats Navarro or Miles Davis played the most shit to the background music of Lloyd Price singing, "Lawdy, Lawdy, Miss Clawdy." This place was jammed up tight with uniformed and civilian-slick airmen, also shouting and laughing at the top of their voices. And while Estrella was a predominantly black bar, there were white and Latin troops hollering with the Bloods, insulting each other, bullshitting each other, sympathizing with each other, trying to make it and do their various hitches.

"How the fuck you get Ray to come into town, Laffy?" White was standing tall and dour as usual, slightly tipsy and bending toward the new arrivals. "How the fuck you get . . ." he trailed off, giggling. "Yodo, buy Ray a drink for coming off the base."

Yodofus T. Syllieabla (Carl Lawson's chosen moniker to evade the constant depression of being an Air Force medic for seven years of his life and having still only one stripe) was a very yellow-colored fellow, and with the booze in him he had colored slightly red, blinking his eyes. "You want Yodofus T. Syllieabla, the High Priest of Swahili and the Czar of Yap, to do what?"

"Buy them a drink, silly nigger!"

"Yeh, Ray, why you out here in this dirty town? And in this dirty bar?" This was Bill Perkins, an aspiring photographer from a suburb of Boston. His name wasn't really Perkins, but his parents had changed it in order to get in the suburbs, and Perkins felt guilty about that when he got loaded. So he tried not to get loaded, but it didn't stop him. He got loaded, then guilty, all the goddamn time. "You said you didn't need to come into Aguadilla, but here you are. And with that Groucho Marx–lookin cat. Stand up straight, Laffawiss, goddamnit. You're standing in a hole."

Laffy half-turned immediately. "Hey, Johns, let's get the fuck outta here. I'm not gonna be insulted by guys named Perkins whose names ain't really Perkins. Hey, I wouldn't sell you a pickle on the Lower East Side, my friend. Not even a herring, Perkins. Shit!"

"Shut up, Laffawiss, I wasn't talking to you. Johns, why are you in town with this guy?"

"Aha!" Yodo was pointing the umbrella stick he always carried. "Aha, I know. And Anachronobienoid knows too." Anachronobienoid was the name Yodo had given to his stick. His "all-purpose stick," he called it. The stick had once cursed out a warrant officer who had been staring too long and hard at Yodo. The stick leaped to the fray, making horrible nigger curses that sent the W.O. scrambling down the dusty road outside the PX in Ramey.

"I know, I know. You two are on a secret pussy mission. That's all this Groucho Marx sucker is searching these streets for . . . What?" Yodo held his stick up as if it was talking. "Yes, yes. Anachronobienoid says he's surprised at you, Airman Johns. Didn't know you was into these SPM's. Aha." Yodo's humor always cracked Yodo up the most, and he howled.

"Shut up and buy them a drink, Yodo, goddamnit," White persisted.

"Why are you guys concerned about what I'm doing? You're the kinda guys that give SAC a bad name. That's why Ramey's got the highest venereal disease rate in SAC too. Hey, man, even my AC got the clap."

"In his ear, probably." Laffy was pacing back and forth without moving, Groucho Marx style. "Hey, Ray, I think we got to go before these creeps influence you against sin!"

"These motherfuckers getting ready to sin. I knew it. Lemme in on that shit or I'll squeal!" White had to steady himself on Perkins, who was no more sober but since he was normally stiffer he could play sober better than White.

Pulling Ray Johns by the arm, and exchanging putdowns and jokes and repeated laments, Laffawiss turned and grunted at the weight of dragging Johns out of the bar. But now with wobbly White in less-than-hot pursuit and Yodo waving his "all-purpose stick." White was saying, "Hey, if you guys are gonna start sinning and shit, don't leave me out, you greedy motherfuckers. Don't leave me out, goddamnit."

"Anachronobienoid knows. He will see what you do, no matter where you go!" Yodo shouted, as Laffawiss and Johns hotfooted it out of the Black Star and up the narrow alley street, deeper toward the section known as Mondongo. This was the heavy whore area, and was, of course, strictly off-limits. But in reality, about as off-limits as the day-room candy machine.

It was night now, and although the low starry skies over the enchanted island were bright and clear, still the lights of Aguadilla did not make for very much illumination, and so the streets as they wound also got darker, it seemed, the deeper into Mondongo the two adventurers got.

Johns had on a pair of khaki pants that could have been his class-A khakis, but also a blue-striped Ivy League button-down shirt with the sleeves rolled up, plus the usual dark glasses. Laffy had on his class-A khakis, with his cap tipped on the back of his head. To the question, "Why you wanna wear your goddamn uniform if we gonna go off-limits, asshole? You just wanna get arrested."

"Why should I disguise myself? What am I gonna do, pass for Puerto Rican? Hey, man, people can look at me and tell I'm a Jew from the Lower East Side. I'm telling you."

"Look, man, you got me to leave the perfectly comfortable barracks for some kind of flesh chase. Now you wanna get me busted. Laffawiss, I do not want to get busted. I don't want no Article 15. I don't want no extra duty, no KP, no double guard duty shit. Why did I go for this bullshit, is what I want to know."

And while this was being said, the two wound further and further away from the USAF-sanctioned center of Aguadilla, back down into the center of the off-limits prostitution and gambling sector, Mondongo. Laffawiss was an old hand at winding through these semi-lit, sometimes unlit streets, in search of a little distraction from the day-to-day (and night-to-night) madness of the "war cats."

For Ray Johns, it was a little too exciting, though no one unfamiliar with his generally calm, even taciturn manner would know anything out of the ordinary was happening—he could drive polygraph interpreters crazy. But his heart was actually stepping a little faster, the darker and narrower the streets got. The further away from military tourist unreality they got, another Aguadilla emerged, with even fewer stone and clay houses and more and more low tin-roofed wooden shacks.

It was darker, but probably not as dark as Ray Johns's souped-up senses had it. The streets at first seemed strangely empty, but then as the two soldiers' eyes adjusted to the tightening light, they could see occasional figures sweep past them or just beyond them. They could see people sitting on steps and porches. They could see one or two people stop and turn to regard them as they passed.

"Come on, Johns. Don't get scared. It's just people walking up and down like they do all over the world. No need to get psyched out!" This was Irv Laffawiss,

AF 133 75 9011, Airman Second Class, radio operator, 73rd Strategic Bomb Command, unassigned, speaking. He was urging Airman Second Class Ray Johns, AF 125 60 8040, weather-gunner, 73rd Strategic Bomb Command, Crew N45, to keep marching through the menacing night toward the Golden Bowl.

"No need to get psyched out? I'm not psyched out. I just don't feel I need to get busted. 'Release tension,' he says. Hey, and I didn't even go for it. I was just humoring you, old man. I just thought you needed some company down here in the boonies."

Laffawiss kept on trucking, head poked forward and tilted a little downwards, a modified street-Groucho. "Oh, man, you can lie. Don't panic. Just don't panic." And they kept moving into darker Mondongo.

"You mean you have so little self-discipline . . ."

A few people scattered out of their way as they pushed on. They saw a couple of tall, red-faced obvious G.I.s in loud "civilian" clothes poke their heads from behind a shack and wave at them. Though if they'd stopped to talk to those two troops, the four of them would have been rolling in the dust after exchanging a few paragraphs as to the nature of reality in general.

"You mean you have such little control over your pecker," Johns picked up, "that it can demand that you trail around back alleys all night?"

"I know, I know," Laffawiss shot out. "You may prefer Merry Fist. You keep pullin on that thing, Johns, it's gonna fall off."

"You keep messin with these nasty whores, yours is gonna turn green and rot off." The two G.I.s laughed, too loud for their purposes. "And I'm speaking," Johns added quickly, "as a noted microbiologist!"

"Don't make so much noise." Laffawiss slowed a bit. It seemed there was no light at all. Some flickering matches, muffled laughter close and fading, unknown movement. Overhead, the moon and the stars and some scattered clouds, and somewhere, the hint of ocean.

Laffawiss came to a full stop, with Johns bumping into him in the dark like in a Charlie Chaplin film. Laffy stood stock-still for a few seconds, till Johns pulled at his sleeve, whispering sweatily, "What the fuck is going on? Do you have any idea where we are?"

"Hey, I know this routine cold, Johns. Don't worry, it's OK."

"OK, my ass. What the fuck's going on?"

Another few seconds, and a man appeared in Johns's eye who was already talking in hurried whispers to Laffawiss. Johns jumped inadvertently as the image came in, but he poked his head toward the two to try and hear what was going on.

Laffawiss reached back for his friend, smacking him on the shoulder. "Come on. This guy's taking us to the women. See how quick that happened?"

"Who's this guy, Laffy?" Johns tried to look in all directions, but it was totally black except for indistinguishable shapes and noises. "What's he, a pimp or something?"

"Yeh, yeh. Now shaddup before you scare the flesh away."

The three men walked perhaps a hundred yards, up one alley and down another. In a minute or so, Laffawiss was leading Johns up three steps and across the short porch of one of the wooden tin-roofed shacks, completely sheathed in darkness. Laffawiss knocked at the door and almost immediately it swung open.

There was a candle or oil lamp lit, and it amazed Johns how much light was in the room that could not be seen from the street. He could not be sure that there were windows. The walls were pasted up with pinups from various Puerto Rican rotogravure sections. But it looked like the *New York Daily News*, with open-legged blondes, &c., though modest by today's standards.

In the room was a table with chairs, a few notches below your local corner ghetto "furniture" store. A woman had opened the door. And she stood now, in some hopeless, colorless cotton housecoat-like garment, without shoes. As Johns's eyes adjusted to the dim lamp, the hair on his neck rose and shivered in stiff formation. The woman was old and hideous. She was like some kind of "witch." The word slid uneasily out of Johns's mouth and punched his comrade in the back. This was followed by Johns's actual hand poking Laffawiss in the small of his back as he leaned forward to half-whisper in half-Spanish pidgin the desired relationship.

"What?" Laffawiss was showing fingers to the woman, indicating the market value of the *chocha*. He was trying to complete the deal, in a fairly circumspect way. He did not need to be bothered by his stuttering friend. So at the next poke, he half-wheeled around. "What?"

"That witch is ugly as shit, Laffy."

"Two dollars, short time." Laffwiss was talking to the old woman again. "Three dollars, long time." The woman was nodding her head vigorously and making the two- and three-finger signals back to Laffy.

"Hey, Laffawiss." Johns was still trying to whisper, but not really succeeding. "You bring me all the way down here through the goddamn AP's for this, you fucking pervert?"

"This ain't the woman, Johns. Jesus H. Christ, you think I'm sick?"

"Yeh, I think that."

The old woman now had her hand extended. She was speaking most of the English she knew. "Two dollar, short time. Three dollar, long time."

"Short time, long time?" Johns looked at the woman and shuddered very openly.

"*Mi amigo no comprende. Que es corto vez?*" Laffawiss felt he was speaking good Spanish, but he sounded as illiterate to the woman as she sounded to him. "*Y largo vez?*"

The woman squinted, trying to understand the Lower East Side gibberish. Then she said, "Short time, very short. Long time is till you come." She laughed at the idea. There was nothing in her mouth but memory.

"Laffy, I don't like this a hell of a lot. Where are the goddamned women? If this ain't the one we supposed to lay with—"

"OK, OK, unbeliever. Good *chocha* coming up." Laffawiss was grinning, but the old woman simply stood her ground with her crippled hand extended in the traditional collection position.

"Hey, look, we gotta get the *chocha* first," Laffawiss said. "Let us get the women first, then we pay." He winked over his shoulder to Ray.

"Short time? Long time?" The old woman took a step back and turned toward what now seemed to be another door at the back of the shack, still squinting cynically.

"Long time, yeh. You *know* me. You remember me, Irv?"

"What are you, a fuckin nut, Laffy? Telling this bitch your name?"

"Hey, I'm an old customer. I gotta see the merchandise before I shell out big bucks."

The old woman repeated Laffawiss's first name. "Irv? *Sí, Sí.* You here before. OK, OK. Come on." She beckoned the two to follow, and the gesture made Ray Johns think even more of witches.

On the other side of the back door was a smaller room with one bed in it. The room was almost completely dark, but there was a small candle stuck in a bottle. On the wall was a gold and ivory plastic reproduction of Christ hanging on the cross, bleeding down into the bed. Because even in the dark, the spotted bed sheets, if they could be called sheets, could still be perceived.

Sitting on either side of the bed were two women. They seemed younger than the old woman. But it was going to take a few seconds for the soldiers' eyes to adjust. The old woman still had her hand out, but Laffawiss's determination seemed to influence her.

"Here, see," the old woman said. "Beautiful!"

Johns's squinting eyes began to see the two women as more than vague shapes in the darkness. And no, they were not beautiful. As they became visible, Johns was trying to clear his throat so words could come out.

"Laffy!" It was like a low, but sharply rising moan. "Laffy, Jesus Christ, man," Johns was pretending to whisper. "Are you that hard up, man?"

Laffawiss had succeeded in cooling the old woman out. Their prey was near. Why was this bastard, Ray, trying to queer the deal? "What? Hey, Ray, it's about to happen, man. Don't fuck it up."

"About to happen? Hey, man, they're . . ." Johns wanted to say *ugly*, but he couldn't bear to.

"What's the matter, Johns? You choosy? Goddamn, man. Once you get it in, you won't know the difference. So they're not bathing beauties. What the fuck you want for three bucks, man! Lena-fuckin-Horne?"

"Jesus Christ, Laffy. Jesus Christ." In reality, the women were not as ugly as the old woman, and they were a few years younger.

"Don't worry, Ray. Don't worry. It ain't the looks, it's the movement." Laffy thought this was funny, and bent a little, Groucho-style, one arm hung at his side like he had a cigar. "It'll be great, man. Great, don't worry. I bet you anything you'll fall in love." And at this, Laffawiss almost fell down laughing.

"OK?" the old woman asked, and she started to leave the room.

"Say, man, there's another room back here? Which woman you got and where's the other room?" Johns turned beseechingly to the old woman and babbled the pidgin Spanish he knew. *"Otra cuarto, por favor?"*

The old woman shook her head, about to back out of the room. "No, no," still shaking her head, and pointing at the single nasty bed that straddled the shadows.

"Hey, man, only one bed?" Johns howled. "How we gonna do that, Laffawiss? Shit, one bed? Man, you crazy!"

"Oh, come on. Just lay on the bed sideways. You'll have to let your legs dangle off."

"*Let your legs dangle off?* Goddamn, you ain't even got the normal positioning and shit happening. I didn't know you people from New York were some kind of freaks. Same bed, and let your legs dangle off? Man, how we gonna do anything in the same bed? Don't you even want no privacy?"

This would have cracked Laffawiss up, but he blew air through his teeth instead, moving toward one of the women, both of whom were still seated.

"How you get that one?" Their eyes had now fully adjusted, and it did seem in the dark that Laffawiss was getting the best of the deal, but only by a whisker.

"OK, Ray, you goddamn pest. You take this one. Gimme the other one. It don't make too much difference in the goddamn dark, you know."

"It does to me." They crisscrossed in front of the bed. Laffawiss was already unbuckling his belt as he moved forward, a wide shit-eating grin growing where his face had been.

"Goddamn. Goddamn," was all Ray Johns kept mumbling as he approached the woman who looked like she was in her hard thirties but who was actually only twenty-seven. Johns was twenty-two, Laffawiss twenty-four. "Goddamn. Goddamn."

For some reason, Johns was determined to go through with it, but the whole deal had cooled him out as far as having any raging animal passion that had to be pulled off by some anonymous *chocha*. Laffawiss, on the other hand (and on the other side of the bed), quickly pulled his pants down, and without the least *adieu* got to righteous work, pumping away at speeds sometimes approaching the sound barrier.

Johns was still fumbling and trying to maneuver the woman in some kind of way. And at the same time, trying to remain oblivious of his partner three inches away heaving and wheezing like a small white Groucho Marx gorilla on loan from the Lower East Side.

Not long after, Laffawiss's "long time" was got to in a relatively short time. But at this point, Johns was just beginning to feel that maybe in a little while he might actually begin to feel something—at least be a little more comfortable. And the woman was not giving much help. Instead of going through a few of Scheherazade's 1,001 sexual variations, the way the old soldiers said it was done for them at bases all over the universe, this less-than-plain woman lay back in the shadows and scowled. After a while of Johns's aimless pushing, she ventured, "You finished? It's long time."

Ray was raising his head to make some comment to the babe, and he saw Laffawiss's narrow butt rising up. *What a sight that must be*, Johns thought, *black and white butts flagging away in unison—shit, it's what Civil Rights is all about, goddamnit.*

But then Laffy started sounding like the babe Johns was supposed to be banging. "Hey, Ray, you finished yet? Huh?"

"What? Am I finished? Goddamnit, Laffy. Nobody told you to be so goddamn quick. You like a kid—wham, bam, thank you ma'am." All that to hide the fact that in this surrounding, there was nothing going to happen with Ray Johns. In fact, he was laying there mostly embarrassed in the near dark, wondering how the fuck he'd gotten talked into this madness.

"You finished yet, Johns? We can't stay here all night, you know. Not only are we off-limits, but we only got about forty-five minutes to get back to the base."

"Aw, fuck that." Johns had his head cocked to one side to talk to Laffy, who had now risen up completely away from the woman. "You bastard, I don't care about all that shit. Ain't nothing happened with me yet, goddamnit."

"Hey, you finish now," the woman puffing under Johns called out. "You pay for long time, but not for all night. You finish now."

"Goddamnit, I ain't finished. Laffy, look, you got this bitch throwing me on the floor and shit. I ain't got my money's worth yet."

Laffawiss looked at him and tried to make a suggestive face. But in the half-dark, Ray couldn't tell what he was making faces about. So Laffawiss whispered, "Hey, we didn't pay, ya creep. We'll get our clothes on, then lam outta here. See, you get a little free stuff."

"I didn't get nothin' in the first goddamn place."

"You finish," the woman repeated once more. "Your long time is over."

Laffawiss was pulling up his pants now. Johns had been put off the woman as she tried to rise. Laffy was making faces, urging Johns to get his pants on and make ready to dash out of the joint. But Johns was still reluctant, feeling cheated, even though he and his buddy were getting ready to cheat these women (and their pimp). But then the woman that Johns had been riding stood all the way up and began talking to her companion, who had also risen. Ray Johns could see her now more clearly, and in near profile he saw that the woman was a cripple. She had a large hump on her back. Johns's skin felt like pins and needles, and all he could think to do was shout at his buddy who was about to break out the front door. "Laffy, you dirty son-of-a-bitch! Goddamn you, goddamn you!"

As he was answering Johns, Laffy was pulling his buddy's arm to get him to move. "Come on, Ray. Let's get the fuck outta here."

Johns did not really believe Laffy would run away after fucking the women. It never occurred to him that you were supposed to pay even if nothing happened. But now, after being jerked by Laffawiss, he found himself staggering out into the front room and past the startled old woman, who now had her broom raised to stop the two retreating thieves.

The two women in the back room bust out too, the three of them screaming, "My money, *mi dinero. Mi dinero, maricón! Cholito negro!*"

Then the old lady started calling a man's name. "Miguel . . . *Cabrón!* Miguel!"

Laffy and Ray plunged headlong into the darkness. Laffawiss knew generally the direction he was heading in. Johns knew nothing, except that it was dark and now three women and some crazed pimp were chasing them.

Running, as they were, down the off-limits black

streets of Aguadilla—no, Mondongo—made Ray Johns feel absurd. Like he had been Shanghaied into a *Tom & Jerry* cartoon. Laffy, on the other hand, felt exhilarated. The sweaty air laughed around him like his sweaty skin and sweat-soaked uniform. He had his cap in his hand, running in his squatty Groucho Marx gait. The three women had fallen quickly into the far rear, and the pimp was only a step or two ahead of them. The cries of *"Mi dinero, maricón! Cabrón!"* and other untranslatable obscenities sailed along closer to the feverishly retreating G.I.s. But suddenly, out of the darkness, there were other figures next to them, closer.

"Oh shit!" Johns called out, trying to raise his velocity still higher. Laffawiss was actually chuckling, and the sight of this made Ray very angry, but there was not time to do anything but hotfoot it.

The Air Force physical-fitness programs kept Laffawiss and Johns relatively close in their flight, except Laffy was beginning to breathe a little heavier. Johns ran track and cross country in high school and college, and was actually sprinting easily. If he was sitting still he might have been more frightened, but during the chase he saw it as an emotion-tinged physics problem. The bottom line of this was: *You'll never catch me, motherfucker.*

Then, it seemed, several more dudes leaped out of an alley ahead of them, and all at once they were just about surrounded. A hand scraped Ray Johns's face, trying to grab at his clothes or whatever. Laffy was being reached for, and then both of them were trying to break free from many hands and the blood-seeking Puerto Rican Spanish.

Johns twisted, flailing his arms, and put his head down, twisting and diving for freedom. As he began to receive several glancing blows, he broke free and then accelerated to light speed. In the darkness, it was almost impossible to see clearly the faces of the seemingly young men who lunged at them. He moved away and caught a glimpse, still moving, but with someone's hands grasping for him as he tried to round a corner.

Speeding through the dark, Johns careened blindly into a stack of garbage, knocking over boxes, cans, bags. As he regained his balance, he grabbed the lid from one of the cans and bashed it at the threatening shadows as he ran. He was trying to get away, number one, but then thought he should try to circle back behind where they were jumped to see what was going on with Laffy. Yet it was not merely one block he had to circle, but several, in the blind hit-and-miss fashion his running enforced. And it seemed a long time and a long journey, with the voices behind him. Once, he had to swing the garbage can cover at a couple of dudes moving near the edge of an alley. As he passed them, he wasn't even sure they were chasing him. But now they were, for sure. He ran and ran, hoping he still had the right direction.

When he turned the corner to what looked like the narrow little street where the citizens had first cornered them, Johns's heart leaped again as he noticed a blue Jeep of the Air Police, the red light blinking threateningly from its hood. He could see two air policemen, one black and one white, talking to what looked like a huddle of screaming young locals. To one side of the group, the wrinkled old woman stood, adding her two and three cents to the general roar.

Laffy lay up against one of the buildings, turning his head slowly from one side to the other. Somebody (or bod*ies*) had popped him good. Johns froze for a second, figuring if he showed, he blowed. But fuck it, it didn't mean that much. Who cared? A fuckin Article 15, what the hell? He thought this as he came striding out of the shadows. His appearance set the little crowd on *"Vaya!"* and for some reason the old woman wanted to spit at him.

Looking up wearily, all Laffawiss could offer was, "Hey, do any of you sad sons-of-bitches got a cigarette?" He even gestured at the crowd that strained to ice him. *"Mira, dame un cigarillo, por favor."* They howled blood.

At Johns, Laffawiss merely tried unsuccessfully to grin. "Hey, airman, what the fuck happened to you?"

As the A.P.s closed on Johns, particularly because of his ability to move the assembled crowd, he answered, "I went home to jerk off. That was the worst pussy I ever had." And they tried to laugh again.

The two buddies did get an Article 15 as punishment, and the First Sergeant made them paint the exterior of both of the large cement barracks that housed the flying personnel of the 73rd Strategic Bomb Squadron.

Ray and Laffy renewed their friendship after both had left the service. Johns had gotten out early because someone had written an anonymous letter to his squadron commander saying that he was a Communist. He didn't even protest. Laffy got out a few months early on a hardship discharge he had phonied up.

Ironically, the last time the two were together was in New York City, the fond and flying apple of their Air Force daydreams. Coming down Ninth Avenue together, crossing into the Village, they were jumped by a screaming, bottle-throwing mob of young white boys. Again, Johns, with his fabled foot speed, got away, circling a few corners and picking up a garbage can cover as he ran, laughing at the déjà vu of the whole thing. But this time as he rounded the corner, Laffy had already been taken away in an ambulance.

Two guys, who said they were related to Laffy, came by Johns's house a few days later and left an odd message that they had been there. They had also asked the superintendent "what color" Johns was, for some reason. But he never saw them again, nor did he ever see his old comrade in arms.

July 1983

Blank

L C stopped at the corner and looked in a shop window. At whatever, but the reflection caught his eye and startled him. He did not recognize who he saw. The face would not smile. His shoulders were not stooped, but broad. He had a gray flannel blazer and black tweed pants. A thin yellow sleeveless sweater and open collar, gray silk-mixture shirt, tie-less. His brown hair, carefully combed, flattened casually back to his ears. Perhaps a strand or two brushed his forehead.

He stared, amazed. Amazed at what? He was not certain, only that he was surprised at what he saw in the window, stashed between the hats and ties in the store. He looked at his hands. There was a light brownish-red tinge to them, as from the sun. His nails, perfectly manicured. He turned his hands over slowly, at the same time peering closer into the window, trying to see whether his face was lightly tanned as well. It looked like it, like a light tan over an otherwise healthy but very northern European complexion.

Why was he surprised—yes, amazed? He was not certain. Not certain, except . . .

And his thoughts tailed off as he turned from the shop window and stared randomly up and down the street at the breezy walkers crossing and moving at the corner of East 65th and Madison. Perhaps they were shoppers and executives out to lunch. Perhaps . . . And he turned his head in another direction, watched, then turned it back, then turned around.

He was surprised because . . . Now he had forgotten why, but maybe something was wrong with . . . He crossed toward a drugstore on the opposite corner. Maybe he could look closer at his face, if he bought . . .

But a car mirror served his initial purpose. He stopped and peered into it, now seeing his face more clearly than before. It was smooth, clean shaven. There was a subtle aftershave he could barely smell. His gray eyes narrowed slightly as he inspected his face. But then, what was it? What was so strange? Why was he sort of stumped? Or something. Dazzled? Whatever. It was (his hand slid into one pocket and a few coins tapped and rolled against each other; he noticed the Oyster Rolex watch—it was just after 1:00 in the afternoon, the date read September 1) . . . what? There was something pressing in his mind, *against* his brain, from within. Some pressure. But he could not say from what. He patted his back pockets—there was a gray handkerchief, nothing else. He patted his jacket, finding keys in the right-hand pocket. And in the inner breast pocket, he felt a wallet. He slid it out, unfolded it. People passed him, oblivious and perhaps light-hearted. There was, of course, money in the wallet. He fingered the bills lightly, not really counting, but definitely counting. Not much, perhaps $1600 in twenties and fifties. An inadvertent smile he didn't see flirted with his lips and vanished. He slipped the wallet back into the pocket simply, turning at the same time to survey the passing strangers.

But here he stopped abruptly, as if pondering. It was warm and bright, at the civilized edge of summer's swift demise. He had nothing in his hands. In his mind, a question was forming. But he stepped quickly toward a newsstand and looked down at the papers and magazines, confirming the date. It was Wednesday. He glanced innocently at the headlines and a few stories on the front pages. One paper predicted War, another Peace. Another showed the bare breasts of a blond woman with her open mouth, both grimacing and smiling.

Suddenly, he went into the inside pocket again and withdrew the wallet. He fished for the rows of credit cards stuffed into several compartments. There was American Express Gold, Visa, Diner's Club, Carte Blanche, Brooks Brothers, all made out in the name *Close Securities-LC*. *Close Securities-LC* was on each one, but why was he studying these cards? What, was he going to buy something? But that was not it, it was something else. It was not clear. It was not on the windows of the buildings he looked at, scanning easily toward each of the four corners. He had moved perhaps fifty or sixty feet in the last five minutes or so, according to his watch. But there was something bothering him. Everything seemed alright—in order, so to speak.

He was at the corner now and the traffic light was blinking, about to change, with people streaming by him, absorbed in their movement and the flow of midday traffic through the glistening part of the glistening city. He too began to cross as the flow of people eased off somewhat. But then it occurred to him that he had some time to kill, that he had been looking in the window, and also that he did not know where he had decided to go. He thought it would come to him momentarily, when he touched the other side of his jacket, running his hand into the other inside pocket. Here was an envelope, a long business envelope with no writing whatsoever on it. Inside was a cashier's check with the Bankers Trust seal on it for $2.5 million. The check was made out to Close Securities-LC. 2,500,000, as well as *Two Million and Five Hundred Thousand Dollars and No Cents*, was written on the check. Made out to *Close Securities-LC*.

The bank at which the check had been drawn was very close to where he was at this moment. He looked at the numbers on the buildings. The bank was . . . it was across the street, just in back of him. It was over there, just next to that haberdashery. That was the same store he had been standing in front of, where he'd looked at himself in the window. When he'd been amazed that he did not . . .

He turned, and at this point a steel-gray Bentley eased up to the curb next to him and a black man looked out at him earnestly. In a moment, the man was out of the car and around it, almost at LC's side. "Sir?" he began. "Shall I wait, or where would you like to go?"

The black man wore a gray worsted suit and dark-blue shirt with gray silk tie. A small accommodating smile played at his lips and he reached toward the Bentley's back door, ready to open it at LC's request.

"I should go to the bank," LC said quietly, staring straight at the black man.

"Yes, sir. But I thought you'd already gone in, sir?"

"Yes." LC wanted to say more, but he looked across

the street at the bank and then at the envelope which he still clutched in his hand. He put the envelope back in his inside pocket. "Yes."

The chauffeur had his hand on the door handle, and as LC looked at him, the man opened the door easily and held it for LC to enter. With no thought at all, LC entered the rear of the car. There was a small, well-outfitted bar that opened out of the front of the backseat and a small television. There was also a tiny compartment with the day's newspapers.

On the seat next to him was a leather envelope. LC moved his hand toward it expectantly. At the same time, the chauffeur turned to look at him, asking instructions with his eyes. The question in LC's mind, as it finally made itself clear, was jokish but at the same time frightening. *Who?* The word pushed into the connecting slide between mouth and brain, remaining unsaid but felt in the softest part of his voice. There was a rush of words flooding through, but what was heaviest was a fearful thrust of steel absurdity. He realized now that he did not know who he was. He did not recognize the face, the voice, the clothes, the wallet, the check, the black chauffeur, the Bentley. He did not even recognize completely where he was, except what he had seen in fragments shuffled by in the day and sun and light, sensuous breeze. He did not know who he was.

So he did not know where he was going or where he had been. He had no instructions for the chauffeur because he did not know anything about anything. Was it amnesia? Was he ill or crazy? What had happened to him? He was amazed at what he looked like. Happily surprised, perhaps, at the wallet, the $2.5 million check. The car and chauffeur, there among the tall rich buildings.

"Sir," the elegantly dressed black chauffeur was saying, "are you going back to the office as scheduled, or somewhere else?"

"Schedule?" LC was about to say that he did not know who he was, but it sounded too stupid. "Can you open the window, please?" he said instead. He thought perhaps a little more air and time, some of the sun, maybe, anything. But there was no real panic, it was just aggravating. And for a while he had not even understood that he knew nothing, that there was nothingness just a little before thirty minutes ago. Blankness.

But the aggravation was being replaced now by something else, because the chauffeur was asking him to respond. In effect, for him to be someone. Why couldn't he remember? Perhaps he should go straight to the doctor. Thank god for the chauffeur, after all. He, the chauffeur, knew who LC was. Indeed, on the leather envelope at his side (which his left hand nervously covered) were the initials in slight, elegant gold. *LC*. And the chauffeur knew what these initials stood for. He knew who he, LC, was. He even had some knowledge of his schedule, where he, LC, was supposed to be going. "Follow the schedule. That's it." This was soft, but it rose as he repeated, "Yes, by all means, follow the schedule."

The car slid smoothly away from the curb. The chauffeur wheeled it slowly up Madison Avenue without comment. At LC's fingertips were control buttons. He pushed one on the far right, and quiet music rolled into the back. It was made by a violinist and . . . what was that . . . a saxophonist, it seemed. He did not know who it was. Drums and bass came in seamlessly as the sounds throbbed through the car in gentle harmonies. It pulled at him very softly. He rather liked it, but had no idea whose music it was.

As the car rolled up Madison, LC pulled at the leather envelope and picked it up. It was obvious that it belonged to him the way the rest of these things (or the rest of this situation) did. But he'd been too caught in wonder, blank wonder, and an aggravation that perhaps had now turned the corner toward something more stark. As the car took a right turn, he finally drew the envelope up fully into his hands and opened it. There was only a single sheet of paper and a typed schedule on it. At the top of the paper in gold lettering, *Close Securities-LC*. Directly beneath this title, the heading, *Schedule: Sept. 1*. The schedule, his, read:

12pm Bank—Mr. R.
2pm Office—Briefing
4pm Les Arouilles (?)
6pm Home
11pm Depart Watercrest Port for B.

The schedule was initialed A.L., with a *cc:* to J.W. & R.M. The question mark caught his eye. Why was it there? He looked up at the chauffeur, who was moving his head very slightly to the music and looking straight ahead. The music was playing sweetly, but there was no other sound, not even the car or the traffic.

In a few minutes, the handsome Bentley had circled to Park Avenue just above 70th Street, pulling to a stop in front of a very narrow and new looking building that seemed like it was made of metal. The building was not as tall as the other buildings on both sides, and though it was only slightly shorter, its metallic look made it stand apart. It was not aluminum but seemed like highly polished steel, with no bolts in sight. What was even more striking about this piece of metal sculpture that seemed to be a building was that there were no windows. And just as the building itself seemed narrow in comparison with the buildings on both sides, the entrance also seemed very narrow.

There was an understated sign cut into the metal which read, *Close Securities*. The chauffeur exited without looking back at LC, and was quickly pulling open the rear door for him to exit. What was going on? LC was moving to get out, and he was out, but a larger flood of thoughts washed behind his eyes. *I don't know who I am. I don't even know that. But it all seems arranged and orderly. A schedule.* He had the leather envelope in his hand. It may be that all of this would soon be clarified . . . That seemed stupid. He wanted to turn and ask the chauffeur, but he was moving toward the wooden door of the metal building. He was already pushing it, holding it open for LC to enter. LC tried to move as if he was in control, but he was being swept along. He knew nothing except what the chauffeur said, what the check read, and the credit cards, the money, the schedule. He glanced at the street signs as he passed into the building, and it occurred to him that he did not even recognize the streets. East 70th and Park. The newspapers had said *New York*. He recognized *New York* as a word, a geographic location, but he had never been there. He had no knowledge of New York. He had no knowledge of anything.

They had now passed into a lobby, which, unlikely as it might seem, was paneled completely in wood. There were thick rugs somewhat darker than the wood on the lobby floors. On the walls, large abstract paintings matched the wood and the rugs. On one wall, a small tasteful sign: *Close Securities*. And against another wall just before a bank of elevators, a middle-aged man in a gray suit stood up quickly as LC and the chauffeur entered, nodding respectfully.

The chauffeur led the way past the group of elevators to a narrow wooden door at the back of the lobby. They stepped through it and there was a smaller elevator. The chauffeur pushed the button and the door of this elevator slid open. There were two leather jump-seats at the back of the elevator, which apparently could be pulled into place if a rider wanted to sit. But LC could make no independent moves, though when the chauffeur moved to pull down one of the seats, LC made a move with his head that seemed to say that he did not want to sit. But otherwise, the chauffeur said nothing.

The building was twenty stories high and the elevator shot swiftly up, with the lights on the board near its roof blinking as they passed each floor. In a few seconds, the elevator stopped smoothly and the door slid open. The chauffeur stepped out of the elevator, leading the way. They had entered a large room. It was an office, but was outfitted not for any heavy work, but rather to house a presence—a person whose tastes were somewhat intellectual and artistic, and very wealthy.

The taste ran to antique books, wood, Persian and Chinese rugs, and hard-edged abstractions on the wall. There was a highly polished bar and high fidelity components. And for the first time, there was a window. The chauffeur touched a switch and one panel in a wall slid back to reveal a glass-enclosed balcony, somewhat like a hot house with various kinds of flora.

"You want the roof opened, sir?" the chauffeur asked softly.

LC could only nod, and in a moment the glass panels slid away and a cool breeze from the open city swept in. LC moved to the edge of the terrace and looked down at the swirling streets below, across the avenue toward the East River and Queens. The trees on the roof swayed and the air was clear. Behind LC, the chauffeur moved and stepped close to him, holding a drink which he then handed to LC, as if he was expected to.

"You have fifteen minutes, sir. You want me to ring for Miss London?"

What would LC say? He thought. *And what would he say to a secretary?* Maybe she would open up some path to what was happening. It was probably amnesia or something. He did not even know his name. But the idea of a name had not meant anything to him until this moment. Apparently, he was LC and he had some position of responsibility and authority at Close Securities. He could ascertain these things, but they seemed abstract.

They were words, in his head, of some meaning. But they signified nothing specific or ultimately clarifying to him.

He had accepted the chauffeur's offer. This tall, dark-skinned black man in the elegant clothes. The chauffeur, LC noted, was dressed as tastefully as he, but how he got in the clothes he had on was blank as well. He appreciated the things he saw and had on and seemed to have, but still there was a distance between him and all of it, because he understood nothing.

The chauffeur went to the desk and pressed a button. "Miss London." Turning toward LC, he said, "If there is nothing else, sir, I'll be in the outer office at 3:30."

LC nodded, trying to be more positive. But still he said nothing. He wondered if that bothered the chauffeur, but apparently it did not. The chauffeur made a deferential gesture with his head and as he was leaving, a tall middle-aged woman with tinted wire-rim glasses and gray suit with light gray scarf knotted like a tie came into the room. She wore black Cuban heels and carried a leather folder and gold pen. She was smiling as an efficient person smiles to let her boss know that she has completed all assigned tasks and is ready for anything.

"Sir," she said simply, "I hope you are well."

LC nodded, at a loss as how to respond. The woman—her name was London, the chauffeur had said—stopped to open her folder and began speaking like the efficient person she seemed. It was a low, steady, airy voice, like one that could be heard over loudspeakers in airports or department stores.

"Everything is prepared for the meeting, sir. I have the agenda. Nothing special, just the preparation for your trip tonight."

She handed a paper from the folder to LC. It listed four names, and under them in brief sentences the apparent responsibilities they had while LC was on his trip.

"Mr. Wallace, Mr. Edrick, Mr. Costen, and Mr. Wray are all waiting in the conference room. They each have a brief response to the assignments they've been given in your absence, but there seems to be no real hitch. It should go smoothly. Mr. Williams is about to go into the conference room. He'll arrive at Watercrest at 10 p.m. to accompany you. Mr. Scales is finishing up the last tasks he has in that regard, and of course will be waiting in the outer office when the meeting is finished."

The sheet read:

Wallace: Communications between LC and staff and any board members. Project B maintenance.
Edrick: Project B maintenance and development.
Costen: Project C projections and design.
Wray: Normal comptroller functions—special attention to target investment area.

There was a space under this list, then:

Williams: Overview of B trip goals.

"The rest of the papers and charts are here," Miss London said, holding up the folder to LC. He automatically took it from her. He had said nothing at all. He wondered how he looked. "I will see if Mr. Williams has come in and all is ready." She stepped away from LC and slid another panel back in the wall. On the other side, five men sat at a long table in a high-ceilinged room with what appeared to be a slit running around the entire top part of the wall that admitted light. "They are all ready, sir." Miss London gestured and LC, knowing no other course, moved toward them through the door.

The five men—one closest to him (this must be Williams) and the other four ranged around at the far end of the table—all stood and acknowledged LC's entrance. They spoke deferentially and seemed to smile as one, not with happiness but out of mutual knowledge and perhaps security. Miss London followed LC into the room and took a seat by the wall with steno pad in hand, also smiling.

LC was at a loss. Anyone could, perhaps, say the things that would start such a meeting, with the proper background. LC simply placed the folder Miss London had given him on the table, opened it, and looked at the gentlemen closest to him. (All these men seemed in their late forties or fifties, except one who sat directly opposite LC, and the one closest to him LC took for Williams. These two were older. LC was actually around the same age as the three other men, somewhat younger than Williams and the man who sat opposite.)

As LC opened the folder, the man who seemed like Williams took up the calling out of items on the agenda, and each man in turn discussed what was outlined. All of the men in the room looked similar.

They were dressed in dark suits (with some diversity according to taste or whatever—however, not much) and none of them looked at all "ethnic."

LC was fascinated at the reporting that went on. Williams made a few corrections, additions, extensions, but for the most part all was straightforward. Of course, LC had only the vaguest idea of what they were talking about. He must have had some training in . . . something. He must have some background. But he did not know it. He did not know anything but the surfaces of things. Words without substance, with invisible contexts.

But then why sit and go through with all of this? He could understand to a certain extent some things as they unfolded in front of him. Close Securities was an investment firm, he gathered. These men were high officers in that firm, reporting to LC, who was going on a trip. The place "B," which was LC's destination, he could not even ascertain from the reporting. But from Williams, who seemed to be his closest assistant, "B" was not too far away. The firm's Learjet would take them there. It was a combination of business and relaxation. A deal was to be cooked up with a bank and local investors in "B," and Williams would do most of the work with LC there to provide the image of Close Securities' highest commitment to the project, but at the same time he would be mostly relaxing. Or so it seemed.

Why did LC let it go on? He was fixed in the chair staring at one, then the other, fascinated by a life in which he was a central, even controlling figure, but of which he knew nothing. He had said nothing at the table. He had said nothing at the meeting. He nodded at a couple of witticisms but doubted whether he had smiled. He remembered the face in the glass did not smile, and that seemed strange, amazing. It alerted him that something was out of whack. Yet the talk went on, the business, the slight humor, the deference. Was it simply his face and body that commanded this obvious life of power and luxury? Nothing moved through his mind but blankness and questions about blankness. He knew what these people said, but only a trifle of it. And that was his entire fix on reality. The talking and smiling went on. Was he always going to be like this? Perhaps if he stopped them now and told them the truth, he could be cured. For the first time, he acknowledged that he must be ill, or else all these other people were. But they know who they are. They are performing their tasks efficiently and happily. *I am in darkness, with no road in or out*, he thought. This could not go on. The game had gone far enough. So he began to talk.

"I cannot remember my name or who I am. Everything is blank and dark, with no way in or out. I found myself in front of a shop window and didn't even recognize who I was. My face in the glass startled me. I would have wandered away, except the chauffeur picked me up and brought me here. I have no knowledge at all of what you are talking about or what my role here is. I have no information or memory. It is all blank."

At this, LC threw up his hands in a gesture of futility and waited. But everyone in the room was laughing. As he stood and made a broader gesture of futility, they all stood and laughed even harder and pounded each other on the back. Even Miss London stood and laughed, though with a certain deference. Williams took LC's hand, shaking it to show how effective his statement had been. They all stood laughing and addressing each other at LC's statement. And then they started to move out of the room, still delighted with it all.

Second Ending

After the others had left, Miss London moved the door so that LC could go back into his office. She quickly made him a drink and just as quickly opened the door to her office. The chauffeur, Scales, stood up as she entered. LC did not know what the drink was. It was brownish. He tried to look at the bottle she had poured from. It was Scotch, into which she had put water and ice. But LC knew nothing of drinking.

Scales stepped forward and LC acknowledged his presence by downing the drink. It was warming and calming. The events of the boardroom had sent his head spinning a bit. He had not known how to react so he said nothing, merely looking from one to the other of his laughing apparent-colleagues. His dilemma was humorous to them. It might be humorous to LC as well, if he could carry it correctly, he reasoned. But still, he had grown more and more uncomfortable, not knowing anything. And when he'd said this, it sounded ridiculous. Perhaps if he had used the word "amnesia," they would have taken him more seriously. That's why such words exist—to make experiences seem more readily disposable.

Scales carried an attaché case in his hand with LC's

initials on it. "Mr. Scales has all the documents, sir." Miss London extended her hand. "Have a good trip. We will take care of everything."

LC could only nod and pump her hand, as if acknowledging what it meant. He had said literally nothing but the truth, and it had contributed some light humor to the events, nothing else. At no time had he said anything to hide anything. *It is like a story I read,* he thought. *Yes, a story.* And that thought fascinated him, because for the first time there was some vague shadow of a past or an identity. *Some story I read,* he thought. *What story? Where? And who read it?*

As Scales and LC descended in the private elevator once more, LC figured there was a way he could get more information before opening up again. This time he would say "amnesia," and they would take him seriously.

"What goes on in here?" LC asked Scales.

"Where, sir?"

"In this building we're in. In these offices on all these floors."

Scales looked momentarily puzzled. He replied, "You want to stop on a certain floor, sir? Would you want to walk through a floor of offices before you go? You want me to contact Miss London?"

"No. I want to stop now on any floor—just to look. I want to know that, at least. I want to see."

"Yes, sir." Scales pushed a button on the control panel. The elevator stopped smoothly and the door slid open soundlessly. Scales held his hand against the door so that it might not close inadvertently. They stepped out into a long paneled corridor which seemed doorless, yet at certain points there were narrow glass slits which apparently enabled one to look though to the other side of the walls.

"What is this?" LC wanted to know.

"Uh, this is the third floor, sir. There are production rooms here, of course."

"Production?" LC wanted to know more and see. "Let's go in one."

"Of course." Scales moved smartly but not too quickly up the hall. He pressed a button and a panel slid open in the wall, so that they could enter. Another step and LC would be at the opening, but he glanced through one of the slits as he moved toward it. There were many people moving back and forth, seeming to pick up . . . something. But he had already gotten to the opening and Scales stood at one side to let him enter. At the door, a middle-aged man with thick glasses immediately jumped to his feet from a desk place, in such a way as to command the entire large room that lay beyond the door.

LC had expected an office or series of offices. Instead, there was one huge room, though the walls were curved in odd ways so that he could not see all of the room at once. On the desk of the man that had stood up with great deference were a series of monitors that enabled him to see throughout this room and what seemed like other large rooms on the other side of this one.

There were maybe two or three hundred people in the room where LC and the two other men stood. The people were divided into small gatherings of about twenty to thirty. Men and women of varying nationalities, it seemed. Each group hovered around, bending and scooping and placing things in sacks which they had on their shoulders. LC could not understand what they were doing. He moved tentatively forward.

"Is there something specific you're interested in, sir?" the man with the thick eyeglasses asked. "Any particular production group?"

LC shrugged. "I just want to know what they're doing." He thought he sounded apologetic, but to the man in the eyeglasses he must have sounded deadly ironic. The man moved quickly forward toward a milling group, who seemed to see nothing but the . . . It was scraps of paper they were picking up. Scraps of paper being pushed out of . . . It was difficult for LC to see. He moved a little closer, Scales at his side and slightly behind him.

"Sir?" Scales asked. But LC said nothing. He took another step.

The man with glasses had said something to someone and the closest group seemed to open a bit so LC could see more directly into the center of the milling and moving and scooping. There was a machine with a screen of some sort. Numbers flashed up and across the screen as LC came forward still closer. Numbers and names—cities, it seemed. LC could not see it all, but out of the machine's "mouth" shot a steady stream of papers, scattering in all directions. White papers blown out, it seemed, as the numbers and names registered across the device.

"The I-90 computer, sir!" the man with the thick glasses said. But their talking did not distract or divert the milling men and women, who scrambled patiently and without expression to pick up the papers, putting them in the bags. LC wanted to see what was on one of the papers. Why were they being shot out and picked up like this? Was this efficient? He wanted to ask this, but as he readied his mouth to speak, a bulky blond man came into view on the other side of the crowd. He, like all of the others, had on a dark suit and tie. But this man wore dark gloves as well and he carried no bag on his shoulder, but in his hand was a long blue tube with what appeared to be red flashing eyes on either side of one tip.

As LC slowly scanned the room, he could see that at each *station*, as they were called, near the center or edge of the milling crowds, was a similar figure, wearing dark gloves and carrying the blue tube with the red blinking eyes. LC looked toward the man with the eyeglasses as if for some further explanation, and the man tried to smile with the smile of the employee at your service. Scales stared straight ahead, looking at the groups but somehow not focusing directly on them.

At one point as LC stared and was about to turn and ask or exit quietly—he could not decide which—one of the people almost directly in front of him stopped scooping and stuffing and froze in his tracks. It was a large man, one who had seemed most energetic in catching and scooping and stuffing. He was frozen stock-still, almost like he wasn't breathing. Then, almost as suddenly, he started to sag slowly, very slowly, like something melting or having the wind slowing sucked out. Now the man with the blue tube moved forward and touched the big man with it. The thing's red eyes sputtered furiously and LC thought he heard a brief humming. At once, the big man rose up as if he had never stopped, and resumed his catching and scooping and stuffing. No one seemed to even notice it.

LC wanted to question, but he knew that was foolish. He had been at the top among the most powerful (and the most informed), he presumed, and they had laughed. *I know now it is amnesia. It must be something like that. I don't know anything about any of this.*

In thinking so deeply about his problems, he inadvertently jerked his head and arms in a manner that suggested to Scales and the man with the eyeglasses that he wanted to leave. They both turned and strode forward to lead him out of the production room.

"Is there anything else, sir?" the man in the eyeglasses asked. LC shook his head. Scales moved to the door and made it slide open. He stepped out into the corridor and LC followed.

After a few steps toward the elevator, LC, figuring there must be some way to find out more, asked, "Do *you* know what goes on in there?" As if he was checking to see Scales's understanding.

"Yes, sir" was the chauffeur's reply. "Information. The production of information." Scales smiled at his precise answer, but in a non-irritating way. He had the door to the elevator open now. LC entered and said nothing. He was thinking about amnesia. About not knowing anything. About how he would get out of all this blankness.

"Will you be going to Les Arouilles, sir, or directly to the house?"

If I go home, LC was thinking, *perhaps there will be something recognizable, something that will reconnect me with myself. It is not that I reject anything in this world, but I must reconnect up to it in consciousness.* "The house" was what he said, following the chauffeur through the lobby and out into the street, where the rear door of the Bentley was quickly opened. LC got in and turned on the stereo and fixed himself a Scotch and water with one piece of ice.

As the limousine moved quietly along the streets, through the tunnel and up the turnpike into wooded, peaceful, pastoral New Jersey, LC relaxed, letting his questions maraud inside his head without trying to draw conclusions or resolution. Finally, he drifted off to sleep, a puzzled gray sleep with no dreams and no answers.

Third Ending

When LC woke up, the Bentley was cruising up a grass incline, on a narrowing road which quickly reached its top and leveled off. The road was sided by large rocks every five yards or so, natural but whitish. They seemed to get larger and larger, until they got larger than humans as the road pierced straight ahead and entered what seemed like a forest of tall, very straight trees. It was now late afternoon and the sun was cascading through a reddening sky, the tall trees suddenly hiding the light, with gray shadows made to look stranger by the reddening tint abstracting the shapes of everything.

But the car came out of the forest, which seemed now simply a grand fence around the low, wooden windowless structure that lay just ahead, behind a freeform fence of huge boulders, like those lining the approach road. The windowless house was made of some dark wood, though a thin strip of light-admitting glass ran around near the roof.

The house was placed in the middle of a formal garden, but the garden seemed not so much a garden as a wild mixture of improbable-looking trees, shrubs twisted like Japanese bonsai, and high bushes with red flowering bulbs—the flora of some specialized collector. LC watched impassively, the images flowing through his eyes and mind, colliding painlessly with his questions. He sat up, and the chauffeur acknowledged this by raising his eyes slightly in the rearview mirror, but said nothing. The Bentley moved forward a few more feet, then veered to the right. The land rose a little but was mainly flat and set out with flashy flora and large stones, the road carrying them around a curve so that they were headed to the side of the house. There was not a gate or place to enter at the front, but one could simply walk through the openings between the stones. At the side, the road turned into an opening, which led behind the stones and dipped down toward the entrance of a garage built right into the house.

The garage door swung open as the car approached, and the Bentley rolled in quietly, the door closing slowly behind them. In the garage were three more cars, but LC did not know what kind they were. All except for one looked new. There were several doors or panels around the wall of the garage, which was perhaps as large as a couple of tennis courts. And beyond the area where the cars were parked was a glass-enclosed lounge with all the accoutrements of an exclusive club bar.

Scales had the door open, and LC without a pause

got out. LC tried looking at Scales but did not know how to look. He thought perhaps he could look like he wanted something, like he had some need Scales could fill. But he was a closed container, containing blankness, only questions. And what curiosity he had, though whetted by the twists and turns and newness of everything, was like a rope wrapping him tighter and tighter in its embarrassing absurdity.

Scales caused one panel in the wall to open and they entered the lounge. Scales moved to an elevator at the far side and pressed a button so that the door slid open. It was all wood and leather inside. LC stepped in, Scales behind him, and the elevator hummed upwards. In a moment it stopped and the door opened. LC hesitated, but walked through into a large, well-lit room that seemed to be made, on all four of its surfaces, of the same dark wood. It was some kind of library, office, drawing room—complete with mostly French and English Impressionist paintings, not prints, with the floors set off exquisitely with Persian and Chinese rugs.

At each wall, glass and wood cases showed antique books, first editions. There was a low desk, empty of everything except a control panel for lights, doors, windows, and the expensive sound equipment and various kinds of film projectors and television screens recessed in the ceiling. There was, of course, a bar, and LC, who had no recollection of ever drinking, suddenly wanted a drink. That's what he'd do—he'd speak directly to Scales and ask for a drink. He'd practice what he obviously had been . . . was. And perhaps with practice, what that was—is—would come back. He wondered momentarily if this man he was had any special skills to be in this position. Suppose, he thought, conjuring further with this panicked train of thought, that because he could not remember what that special skill or information was that provided all this (his eyes swept the room now, almost sensuously), could it be taken away? But there were files, reports, minutes. There were ways to reeducate himself. He felt somewhat restored, though thought and counter-thought had both transpired in the split second of his eyes' travel over the walls, floors, rugs, drawings, bar, &c. *I can learn anything*, he thought. *I must be this person they all think I am. It's simply that I have amnesia. But I need a drink.*

Turning sharply to give Scales this order, LC was confronted with an image that was even more shocking than his own reflection in the shop window several hours ago on the street. For the black chauffeur, Scales, now stood just a few feet from him, his legs a little apart, as if planted. His vague accommodating smile was replaced in his dark skin with the mouth of a straight line. LC could no longer see Scales's eyes. The lids were drawn down so tight that only a slit of eye showed. But strangest of all, in Scales's right hand, now pointed directly at LC's stomach, was a modest but nevertheless menacing automatic pistol.

1985
(Originally published in Callaloo)

Tales of the Out & the Gone

Northern Iowa
SHORT STORY & POETRY

The short story should be a sacred form, since it's the most common way we tell our lives. That's why, in my opinion, the most effective kind of story is short indeed, very short & pointed. Short enough & pointed enough to make your teeth curl.

Check Ousmane Sembène's *Tribal Scars*. The flat acrid mystery of it. A world appears, it turns a few times—these turns are called revolutions—and then it disappears. It does not *cease to exist*. It goes somewhere else. Another dimension is a good explanation. Someone borrowed my book, but the mysterious unwinding remains even when disappeared. In fact, you hear me passing some of this on to you. It reappears inside your head, making revolutions.

One short story I wrote insisted itself into review years after a friend laid it on me. And when it returned, it was as some kind of self-defining legitimization of myself for my most constant audience—that group behind the eyes.

It was like this, and dig the dimensions of this whole retelling as another reappearance: I was riding in an airplane going somewhere, logically enough. But in that enforced reverie, perhaps to read poetry or speak, I somehow began to formulate the idea that I could do something different. I guess that was it, something like that.

I was telling myself, *If I want to make money writing, I can do it*. My (nonexistent) God, what a sad idea to be stuck with! *If* is very Dante-esque. Something like a religious concentration camp. I was concentrating on a very campy idea.

I thought, *Hey!* (Perhaps there was no *Hey!*) *If I want to make money writing, I can do it. For instance* (there was no *for instance*), *if I . . . no.* I thought, *If* (again?), *if I wanted to . . . I bet.*

I thought I could write a commercial story. (What an idea! What would that be?) In that frame of mind, I knew that if I wanted, I said to myself, I could get a story in *Playboy!*

And that is when I made a kind of bet with myself. My lips might have moved. Sometimes my lips move when I read to myself silently.

So this story an old friend told me many years ago at the Cedar Bar jumped out of the black hole, as needed. I sat there in the plane and wrote the story exactly as I remembered it. Because I felt such a story was just the kind of "thing" that 'boy would like to play with.

It had everything: mystery, reminiscence, sex (*Maronna mia!*). A guy walks into a bar, tells me a murderous true tale, and I finally write it out years later, in an airplane going wherever. You see how the tale was carried, in many levels and dimensions.

And it proved out. Barely ten days after I passed it to the agent, he sold it (you bet) to *Playboy*. It was called "Norman's Date."

What was it about? Well, the punch line was this guy wakes up with this new love in the middle of the night after frantic lovemaking, and the woman is sitting over him with a pair of scissors in her hand.

So I know there are levels of that, alright? But it was a story. A short story. I called my 1st book of short stories *Tales* in the grand literary tradition, but also because that's what my mother called my excursions away from the truth. They meant *reality*, which has more troops. But they called such digressions *tales*, like de Maupassant.

The dedication to my sister Kimako in *Tales* read, *To Lanie Poo, who's heard boo-coos* (our black French for "a bunch").

And that's the sense of it for me. Tales, or even tails, the last part of the fact.

At this point is the connection with poetry. Verse is a turn, simply. Like a wheel, it has regular changes. Because they are regular, it is evolution, in a sense. It, that wheel, will disappear eventually, but it is turning in the same place. (But even so, it moves something.)

That verse is literally a *turning*. Except what we *want* is *vers libre*—free verse. Never having been that, *free*, we want it badly. For black people, *freedom* is our aesthetic and our ideology. *Free Jazz, Freedom Suite, Tell Freedom, Oh, Freedom!* And on!

So that verse is the same change. Running changes, just running them, over and over.

Free verse, they say. To mean going through changes and making changes. Syncopation, like they say. Pick up the rhythm. For me, even the real mystery of the story is deep too; I go on, because a story is a place where something is stored. Usually seeds—what you seed is stored. In the story.

In verse, it will come around regularly. It is the wheel. The Human Will. To go into the future, to go forward. Beyond what you see. From see to see. Seven Sees, but watch out for the eight ball, a double wheel. Wheel over wheel, infinity turned upright!

But poetry is the *what*. Like the change—going forward, electrically speaking. (You see, this is funny because I've already gone ahead and put you in it. Some of you know it.)

Not Watts but the What. What is it flowing. Because it does flow. We all are pallets on (or in or as) the flow.

Tears, for instance, are made of water. Salt water. They flow. From the eyes. What see. Ripped, the drops, like waves. You see?

So poetry is cries. The poet or griot pours it out, cries out. Like in Europe they had a town crier. They thought the griot just carried news. But the griot carried olds as news for old news, old knews, all knews.

In Africa, we called ourselves *Djali*. (Perhaps the vibe that Yeats recalled in *Lapis Lazuli:* "Their ancient, glittering eyes, are gay.") *Djali*. Not crying, as griot, to cry out. But *Djali*: laughed so hard tears came to my eyes, or laughed to keep from crying! Ancient glittering eyes. Every one. The eggs, the egos, the for instances. Instant after instant turning, changing, free, the possibility in God's eyes. Possibility is God with 2 left eyes.

And when we do our thing, make it, we say *Djeli Ya.* Like Mr. B. (who some confuse w/me) saying, *Djeli Ya, Djeli Ya, Djeli Ya!* Like that!

The short story is a breath of life. Both dimension and basic function. Like the lungs expanding, retracting. The circle of transbluesent spirit in and out, connected like a wheel, a circle, how we go, our role.

The poet is a basic storyteller and these are the shortest stories. (Hey, not necessarily. People like Browning and Dante and Tolson, God knows, could run that telling on and on. But perhaps that is why it was verse, so it could roll on and on.)

One difference is the dependence on rhythm. The great short story writers use rhythm, of course. I don't think you can make the most penetrating use of language—as content or form—without it being rhythm-sprung.

It is the splitting of the one into two. What follows the one going on. Forward. The eye and the being, the ego and the entity, the woman. (All is womb-sent. Everything issues from the womb, the black hole.)

But the dialectic, the opposites. From woman comes man into woman man comes.

The manifestation (see?) of the eye that sees. The are that bees. The proof. The conclusion. There is Be & At. Two things or one thing and one not thing is the whole.

The heart, for instance. It thumps and the silence is part of the not silence—that is what a whole is.

So the splitting of the endless, which is endless because it does not stop, except its go is only possible because of its not go.

Like speed on the sea is measured in knots.

I'm saying that the short story always exists as water dipped for drinking from an unlimited water, a big sea (a Langston Huge . . .) see (how are I spelling this?)?

To get it out, the water to drink requires we be at that place to dip it.

The rhythm is the dialectic that creates description. Everything is a story. Rhythm is the most basic, the shortest of all stories, the Be & At.

To separate these together, looking, is the open story. The tale. Time & place. Together as flow is the rhythm, the endless story.

So the story wants to make sense. The poetry is what sense is made out of.

Like Pres sd. His solos, the greatest of the players, did all tell a story. They were a story. Pres was the *Djali*, and *Djeli Ya, Djeli Ya, Djeli Ya!*

Poetry *wants*, short story wants something. Something is what poetry is. Short story gives it a name.

June 5, 1994
Rome to NYC (post-Feroni)

The New Recreation Program

Joe stopped me on Broad Street. He reminded me we hadn't seen each other in a long time. Laughter was the punch line to all the stories, like it was a moral judgment.

But one wasn't, and it had a tale attached to it—a death ad.

Feeling, we know, is death's fundamental opposition. Joe looked like he was some kind of salesman. He had a vest w/rolled-up points. The large triangles, a J.C. Penney tattersall, thin and dingy.

"Listen to this, man. I saw a car turning the corner last week. My mother was driving. I mean, she was wheeling, too. Speeding around the corner, laughing to beat the band. I called out to her, and at first she didn't see me. She zoomed off. I mean, *zoomed*, dude, like fast as hell."

Joe laughed again. He was patting me on the shoulder. It was genuinely funny, too.

"But yr mother . . ." I heard myself say, trying to edge in with some inquiry.

"You knew she was dead, right?"

"Dead? No. Oh, man. I'm sorry. I didn't know that." I don't know what I was thinking or about to say, except I didn't think his mother would be whizzing through town laughing. "Dead?"

"Yeh, she died a couple of months ago. The middle of the summer."

"What?" I didn't want to crack the thing open, like ask some reality, you know. Not to be unfeeling, I guess.

"Look at you, man. You just heard me." His laughing was thinner now. Like I had missed the punch line.

"But what you mean? I'm sorry, man. I didn't hear that about your mother. But you . . . saw her?"

He had more in this. It was like chuckling. But appreciative, you know.

"Yeh, now you get to that! And no, I ain't crazy. So don't fix your face to look at me like I am!"

"Hey, Joe . . . What you saying, man? I just want to hear it."

He was a big arc of teeth, tongue, and wet amusement.

"Yeh, I buried her." He took a piece of newspaper from the address book he fished out of his pocket. "See?"

Reading his mother's obituary, I knew, was like a chord, a drumroll for the cruncher. But it *was* something interesting. I'd been thinking about domestic problems, struggles at the job, you know, trying to get priorities focused. Walking downtown to confirm I could still feel anonymous and in motion. Breathing in fall and looking at the faces and colors, measuring all the steps and turns that pressed me, remembering task and ideal.

"Well, what about it?"

"You got me, man. What's the story?"

Now Joe put his arms out, as if steadying me. It was

emphasis for the punch line, I thought. "Yeh, I buried her. People prayed and sang. Then there she was."

"Really? Come on, man. It was somebody who looked like her."

"Hey, man. You telling me I don't know my own mother?"

"Yeh, yeh. But you told me she died. You had a funeral . . ."

"Yeh, that's true."

"I don't believe in no ghosts."

"Ghosts?" He took a dramatic step back. "Hey, man. My mother wouldn't be no ghost. That was her!"

"Yeh, really . . ."

"But dig this." He stuck his head up and forward toward me now. The smile had been replaced with a TV monitor. "She zoomed right back around the corner, stopped, and spoke to me. She waved at me. She shouted at me." I looked at him and shook my head like I believed him, but reserved the right. "Yeh, dig this. She said she was on the way to cuss you out for not showing up at the funeral. Not even the wake."

"I didn't know. Hey, man . . . You know if I knew, I woulda been there."

"She said she was going to your house." He was laughing. "You didn't see her, did you?"

Now I started laughing.

And Joe, at this point, turned abruptly, waving as he continued down the street.

"If you see her, call me. Alright?"

I had stopped laughing. I nodded yes as he kept walking. I had got to the corner, Broad and Market, looking over my shoulder every once and again to watch Joe, but he had crossed the street and skipped up the block.

What is it that drives people to this kind of whack-out, I thought. Maybe he was just putting me on, but it didn't seem like it.

But then, as I waited for the light to change, I saw a maroon Buick pushing like hell up Market Street. Yeh, it was Joe's mother. And she saw me. She was waving, more like shaking her finger at me. Like at some naughty child. But what was wild was that *my* mother was riding with her in the front seat. She was peeking around Joe's mother, and the whole thing seemed to crack her up, too.

I walked out into the street, but they didn't stop. I started calling as they drove away. I had to dance to keep from getting bashed by cars.

I'm sure it was his mother. No shit. For real. It looked exactly like his mother. And I'm sure it was mine as well. I know what my own mother looks like. And we buried her three years ago.

November 1988

Mchawi

Roger Oz was a slender, dark, toothy-mouthed happy dude. When we was in grammar school together, he was always walking by you, coolin' somewhere. "Hey," was all he said. And we, in turn, "Hey'd" him back.

He was always moving forward or back off a laugh. Most shit, it seemed, cracked R.O. out. He never made sure you knew what tickled him. It didn't really matter. When he cracked, we felt funny was happening and cracked up too.

One time, when we did slow to half-hang on the way to what he was heading for, he said he'd invent some shit that would get people happy and make them stay happy as long as they was in the neighborhood.

The only difference when I saw him today is that he said he *had* invented it. But it wasn't happy his invention would get you, but high. "High as a Georgia Pine."

I had heard stories about Roger stumbling all over the Midwest. His high-getting ways were pumped periodically across our alumni vine, graping him very high over the years. Fragmented by time, enhancing the tone of the image into antique warmth. As if, looking back, everything was part of our education to some subjective angelhood.

But this afternoon, arriving on a cloud of laughing-story, the real punch line from that aging joke—like it was just three seconds later. He turned to hip us to his zigzag, past us across the playground.

"But dope got here first, Rog. You invented your shit too late."

He dug that when he laughed like this—full out—it woke up in you, wanting to make you dance. Sort of touching you, like his laugh had hands that could reach out and shake you.

"Dope?" he spun around and bent in gales of syncopation. "Naw, man—I'm into nigger Martians and invisible houses. But dope did make me perfect my invention."

He had a shopping bag and reached into it suddenly, like punctuation for the howl he shredded through his teeth.

It was a pair of sneakers. Black with a red button, like Air Jordans. He held them out for me to check, I guess. I reached tentatively and barely touched the soft metallic kicks. He plopped into a chair, pulling his shoes off his feet, shoving them into the sneakers.

"What's this, man?" I didn't know Rog had left us. "Some sneakers?"

He stood very suddenly, bent, pushed both buttons, and rose steadily and smoothly off the floor. Doing the lone part of "The Boston Monkey," like he did back when we walked the Hill late nights, looking for the party. Then he would leave in the middle. Only a couple times when he got hooked up with some girl would he stay longer, and then he'd get in a hassle taking her out there with no car and evil intentions.

So he's sailing and floating slowly, about four then six feet off the floor, idling around the room. He started singing "Moody's Mood" and gyrated with it, easing back and forth across the room, while my open mouth made the place acoustically innovative.

"Hey, man!" he was singing—signifying, really. "Hey, man!" laughing like he could fall. "Hey, man!"

"What the fuck?" It was really out. We know we're ready for anything. But anything got more going for it than our half-used brains.

"Hey! What the fuck? You . . . you invented that? What the fuck is it, some kind of air column? How does it do that?"

"I got a hundred of them already!" He was dancing a twist, waving and sailing, cackling like an advertising stunt.

"Hey, man!" I was really shot out—Roger in these wild, crazy-ass flying Reeboks.

He spun around, and at the back were some tiny whirling propellers glowing jade green. Spinning like mechanical bird equipment.

"Hey, man! How the hell did you do that?" I didn't know what else to say. Like when the invader enthralled us with a cigarette lighter, he flicked on/off with his thumb to let us know our rulers' omnipotence.

"Getting people high," he whirled. "Hey, man! These things don't even use no fuel. No *fuel!*"

"What? Jeezus!"

"Naw. I invented them, so I made them the way I wanted. They run on thought waves."

"What?"

"Yeh, yeh! You just focus on rising up, and *zip*, you rise. You focus on splitting—you split!"

He drifted close to me.

"So what you gonna do with it?" I was getting frantic in a breathless way.

"You call Jesse Jackson over here. And Minister Farrakhan. I know you know them guys."

"What?"

"Yeh, I want the top black leaders to dig this shit." He spaced the words like a hipster checking Monk.

"Oh, man! Yeh." (Yeh, I thought.) "It would be out to lunch." (Oh, wow!) "Yeh, OK. OK." And I called them.

September 14, 1990

Author's Note
The shoes turned problem quick. 1st everybody who bought em cdnt make em work. Though when those who cd got those same shoes, they wd fly right away.

Then people who sd they was going one place & thought about another cdnt steer them & often cracked up. There were even fatalities.

Rog was even sued by the Civil Rights Commission for reverse discrimination & lost.

But the dirtiest tragedy of all was when the Federal Aviation Administration & Lockheed hired & conspired to frame the brother & got him locked up in Atlanta for life.

1990–91

The Rejected Buppie

History & Science are outlawed
    persons guilty of possession
    of these
    are brought before
    a council
    of cannibals
    verdicts
    of red
        Slobber

L. moved out to Elklock, a suburb of Chocolate City, an all-white upper-middle-class neighborhood close to the big city, encircled and all but hidden by giant oaks. Halfway up a mountain. But then I saw him a few days ago, in White Castle. He looked a hundred years old and fixed all who passed him in a maniac stare that seemed almost electric, yet dull, blank.

As I approached him, he turned suddenly. "Amiri . . . Yeh, I'm back and I don't look good. I know."

He was sad and tired, but he pierced me with this magnetic knife his eyes pushed. He put out his hand to shake, and at the same time took a frayed clipping out of his pocket and shoved it at me.

"See?"

The clipping was from the *Elklock Call*. It showed L.

on the front page. His mouth was open and crude fangs were drawn in his mouth, a tail curled over his shoulder. He seemed to have on a red and black plastic space suit. A bloody hatchet hung from his hand casually. The picture's caption read, *Fiend at Large!*

I didn't know whether to laugh or back up. But it was funny. L. was not a fiend the last time I saw him. And he looked even less fiendlike now, sheepishly peeping at the newspaper in my hand.

"Fiend?"

"Yeh. They say I used spells to remain black in spite of their kindness. They say I was observed dancing a black ritual, trying to evoke the evil James Brown spirit. And that I conspired with the forces of darkness to remain emotional.

"They say I chanted madness and was transformed into a huge black genital of flame. And that I terrorized the citizens by appearing just anywhere suddenly, reeking of nigger spy rhythm. That I had tried to preach the evil cynicism of history and science. That I acted lewdly and illegally in doing this, and exhibited all the characteristics of a serial coon resister. That I chewed the heads off white fetish symbols and spat blood like a judge in a black pointed hat and mask. That I hated what they loved and loved what they hated."

"What?" I didn't think it was a joke. Just stretched out past clock or calendar. "Is this real? It's some nut shit?"

"No. They formed a lynch mob. It was legal. The sheriff headed it. He had a writ, a subpoena, a machine gun, a rope. A head full of drooping tissue, wet with spider shit."

"What? What shit is this? What happened, really?"

"They ran me out of my new house. They set the gingerbread on fire. They tore up the treaties that made us tolerated vomit.

"A little ol' lady shit in the middle of the floor in intriguing patterns. Some of the mob took pictures and scooped up the shit, sucking their fingers as they destroyed the house. They arrived in garbage cans with wheels made of Indian skulls."

The brother was running it like some kind of priest or preacher, like destroyed history could erupt as a slanted colored structure, flowing hot beneath an arctic veil. Experience sounds deadly.

"But it's not the mob. Crazy white people rushing into your house—I could accept all that. Like a statue given to someone as a reward."

Now, you can dig what all this sounded like to me, knowing some portion of what all this is and where it really comes from. You dig? But when strange happens, it be strange to you too!

"But you see, I don't know how much you understand about bullshit."

"I know what I understand." Where he had taken this story was out anyway. The form—and you know in the store, like that—an anonymous fullness.

"People like you, Baraka, said all that garbage about brainwash. I could dismiss all that when it gave me pleasure. I could aspire to be in my world, where I was what I wanted anyway."

"People like me?" He was looking at the television set of my expression and the narrative of my random acknowledgments. Grunts and blowing short breaths.

"But you see, the dumb shit is completely inside it, unexpressed by anything outside it."

"Yeh." What the fuck?

"Yeh." He paid the cashier. "You see, if you really understood America, you would disappear into it and be calm and holy."

"I know." He was television's future.

"But its lie is all the way always in all ways. A lie. I love lies and it lied to me. The truth is what hurts."

When you find people talking to you like this, it makes you want to help them in a way that would've made the discussion never happen. Like bullshit about heart-wrenching or being heart-wrenching about bullshit. I know. But then, I knew he was already something alien. That he lived in a space between what he thought and the actual. I couldn't understand him totally at first—it was a definition that scrambled his speech. Drifted his face into clichés.

"You see, even now I'm not rejecting the experience."

"Experience?" It was like therapy. Even racism was useful as a measure for these guys. *These guys*?

"The lie was that they did not hate me. The lie was that they were ignorant. Bullshit. I saw them behind closed doors, dressed in white sheets, feeding on skinned children. Negro children."

"What?" What can you say . . . I caught a hacked snicker in my throat that would've sounded like a laugh. He had flowed out of his own skin calmly, a yellow and brown puddle, smoking. The skin kept talking without eyes, empty as a pocketbook.

"I knew then that we were excluded. That they felt

we couldn't hang. Couldn't understand their huffy ritual."

"Is this shit for real?" Came half-thrown away.

"That's why they attacked us in the press, because we saw the lie."

"Yeh." This was actually a "guy."

"And you see, some of them knew we could fit. That we could eat the nasty nigger anytime, anyplace, anywhere."

The eyeless skin bent and picked up the yellow-spotted bleeding mess of his insides and slapped it on the scale there at the checkout counter.

The mgr had come out and checked the scale, then gestured to a gray bow & arrow Negro w/white jacket, who sliced it neatly so the flesh and guts would fold, then dumped it in a plastic sack and carried it away.

"I'm going to sue!" He was getting a stack of dollars pushed through his empty eyeholes.

"Yeh," was all I said, turning to leave.

April 1992

A Little Inf

Evolution is the going to the going, where the speed of light is the measure, whereby faster than that which "disappears" from this eye. The five senses are the truncated perception of the animal. The seven senses, the nine senses, are stages of that speed, and wherein we cannot get up to speed, we must start up wherever. In the nine-card molly we have dealt. That is the sun's house. The sun to Saturn and back again.

Hell is the waste, burnt up and "disappearing." That is what that "is" as "self" completely disrealized, i.e., without will, accounting for the future but without one, except as time. The engine, the generator, that engulfing fire.

Time is literally speed, and space is time, as going from wherever. To wherever.

We leave here because we cannot stay. We go where we are taken by what we are. What exists is what is viable to get us wherever. And that accretion of self, information, expansion, revelation is the measure—the placement of where we are and will be.

So that we aspire to humanity in the animal place and mind we are held. The slowness is a measure of how far we have to go, to disappear from this circle-cycle, this Milky Way of keep-on-coming.

That's why Sun Ra wanted to "skip" Mars &c. and

proceed directly to Jupiter. That's what he wanted to know and see. He felt perhaps that by dealing directly with the Jupiter-self, he could use Saturn as a spring-board beyond the Milky Way to the literal "beyond" and not come back around into the nine circle.

If this is hard to understand, I can understand. Computers cd explain a great deal of it. But monkeys have difficulty digging the real deal.

November 1995

Dig This! Out?

Remember when the Blood met us on his doorstep, unlocking the door? He explains that he is not who we think, but he will explain. & when he went in, he started right away. Saying he was a replacement for himself, but from a different planet. Maybe he said "place."

We asked him which planet. He looked at us like we was corny. "Earth," he said. Dig that. "Earth!"

And then he begins to put everybody down, or a lotta people we know, cause we can be in the zoo, calm and employed. As the Animals!

Man . . .

Now he says that this is not Earth, but Dirt. And Humans cannot yet inhabit it! Like it was the jungle and we was all Animals. Or even if we knew about Humanity and dug it, we couldn't go all the way because Animals ruled the zoo and forbid Humanity to develop.

"This is a big cave in the sky. I can see it even where I come from. But we so hip, we can imagine the smell!"

So who is you, was what we was asking.

"I am why niggers never die." Yeh, he said that. And dig this . . .

"I am the Charlie
     Parker

Bird
The Soul
   of
Blackness

  A Tale
    of
    Fire
Exploding
thru Space
   Black
   &
   Flying
tale
on fire.

   Out
     is
     my
       Castle

  Gone
  is my
     Name

Who leaves
burnt lies
beyond the moon

I am from
  where you are
    going

& who you
     will be
   to get there
if you don't die.

In 2031 Christmas
was replaced
by Halloween
     as America's Holiday

     The Jack O' Lantern
and Skeleton
replaced
the Star
     &
Christmas tree

The Devil became
     Santa Claus

& Death was celebrated
instead of Birth.

     Finally, the world
had become A Great Poison
     Cave, with skulls
     & bone crosses
     piled up to the
     edge of the polluted
     endless twilight
     H O R I Z O N
          of

Corpses
which were money.

Afro America
slid we Blue Razor
out we Black Belt
    Sharp
like street light flash
in the cities' collective
    I's
Swift & Rising
in us hand
    like night
        Black &
            Invisible
    in a swinging
        arc
        of
        everything
        over yr head
        Swinging Hard
        Comin
        Down
& where it strike
A Red Star
    of
    Blood."

And having said that, he sits down at the piano
and begins to speak. "Parables. You hip to parables,
right?"

Then he starts to recite very rhythmically, and then

sings. We tried to remember it. (A copy of the transcript follows.)

" . . . out is
gone.

JA   ZZ
Yes

JA (Yes!
The Creating   The is
(Jazz   =   The is
"God"   is
be
Yahweh
Jehova   is

        the signs
    ZZ=Lightning
        The & from the
Sky
The N + J upright + connect

Up   not   m
    ZZ =   Lightning
                 Thunder
                 Shango
                 Electric Sky Jism

    I   =   J   M   move
                         more

Eye	RAR		Are
	JA	=	Yes
	JAH		

A (1st/AM)
eye
A
looking
down."

Since then, we get messages on the box. He saying we can meet whenever we got a question. Or an answer. So we discussin it first . . . you know . . .

1995

Heathen Technology at the End of the Twentieth Century

When they discovered how to remove and imprison the mind (to make the brain unmetaphorical), dis/image it, there was a shrill whoop in the small laboratory. This whoop is repeated each time the process is repeated.

I saw the yellow circle on Jay's forehead and instinctively pushed him away, thinking to misdirect the "Yankee" beam. It worked partially. He developed a love for Robert Bly and Michael Harper and could no longer dance.

He recovered after Red came up with the antidote: Trane and Aaron Douglas eight times a day. And the Babs Gonzales *Be-Bop Dictionary* eye chart to check every hour, with verbal repetition halfway emphasizing the rhythm.

A few years before, if you "remember," before History was 1st defined as nonsense and then outlawed, little Willie came up with the bound metaphor as energy source. If the metaphors of a heavy group were rendered collective and focused on whatever, energy and power could be produced.

Con Edison cops 1st detected the profit drop and

unlisted disd/structs still lit and heated. That was wild and they swooped in, got a criminal blunt jingle to penetrate. They came up with a simulated BM, like rock and roll to the truth, and began to market it once they got a meter for individual heads.

Then they ruled the original an illicit drug and anybody with lights &c. unlisted in the disd was an abuser.

They had copped the fiveness and hummed for scat, limped for real unhip and copped a group of tan Ivy Leaguers to go for real folks, just after Rectum's brother became president. The colored riff nigged the still lit and lit. Clarence was a greenish statue with fecal-perfumed Bibles splashing us on the way to the Under-Mart. His shadow, remember, was permitted to function and they had a silver bullet on his chair which sang slave songs when they killed somebody.

The brain switch began with naked murderer unisex supermodels arriving at certain peoples' houses like Jehovah's Witnesses. The victims were so stunned at the 1st digging that they could be quickly disabled and dismetaphored.

This worked very well till it was discovered that if no TV set was on or no newspapers open, then the supermodels looked like Dahmer carrying a newspaper with his picture on the front page.

That's when the TVs would come on automatically at daybreak, quiet so you didn't know it. And *Dead Peepas Daily* would be slid under your door without a sound.

So then California (the name of the U.S. since 2019. Capital: Dallas) began to sweep metaphor out of citizens' minds large-scale. It was a major project. Every day the mounting aggregate of stolen metaphor metabolism was released with the stock market reports.

The problem began when the collected metaphorical power collectively imagined nothing existed but what it could not imagine.

So like gigantic nuclear-force wheels, the present sped into the future and the past carried garbage across the horizon. No one could be anywhere unless they didn't yet exist. What existed changed and changed. The buildings rotted and the people disappeared. Reappeared. And the people whose metaphor had been stolen could not imagine what was going on. And they disappeared anyway.

So swift had change and transformation become that everything was a blur. A blue wailing blur, like speeded-up flicks. Things, places, persons, nature itself rushed, grew, vanished, was replaced, and everything shook like Saturday-night-nigger-party Bloods spinning on the one.

Red hipped me to all this and we walked around digging like you dug Sun Ra coming out with his hop and chant. It was like Mao said: the world, what is so fantastic, it could freeze you in your digging.

So nothing could exist except everything that rushed and changed. We, with Red's invention, monitored the hip and hung out inside the blue song.

But like a child with a nasty thing inside it which it finally rejects and ejects, the rush spun into another angle of motion and movement. And it seemed places. And with that, soon faces, some wide-eyed "humans," appeared.

We are approaching some of them now. And it seems nakedness is obsolete. They are their own clothes. And they are laughing!

July 8, 1995

Rhythm Travel

Your boy always do that. You knock, somebody say come in. You open the door, look around, call out, nobody there. You think!

But then at once, music comes on. If you watching, there's a bluish shaking that flickers—maybe "Misterioso" will surround you. The music is wavering like light. The room seems to shift, to step.

Then you recognize what you hear, man. "Aw, brother, you at it again. You in here, ain't you?"

A laugh. This dude.

"Yeh, I'm in here. You hear me. You feel me. Here I am." He appears, laughing and pointing at you. "Hey, man. I'm still developing this."

"What you call it?"

"Anyscape. The 1st one. Molecular Anyscape. The Re-soulocator—that was the improvement. T-Dis-Appear. Nicknames. Perfect Nigger. American Citizen. Ellisonic. Migration. I got a name for each step."

"And now?" I rolled my eyes as he got completely out next to me, dissing the Dis report on Appearance.

"This is the next to last. I can disappear. Dis visibility, be unseen. But now I can be around anyway, perceived, felt, heard. I can be the music! Yeh. But now I got something even heavier."

This dude is out—it ain't no jive. He had actually

done those things. And he never swore me to secrecy
either. He just fixed it so I couldn't remember nothing,
except when I came back.

"Further out? The cloth refiner?" He said he needed
to make the cloth fade more so he could get in and out
of the bank w/o any hysteria. It took a few hundred
thousand to get where he was technically.

"How come they don't detect the money splitting?"

"Well, I ain't been able to stabilize the cloth thing.
Sometimes people see the money floating off. But I still
get away."

"How come they don't say nothin'?"

"Well, it's hard to explain, I guess. Floating money.
They studying it."

"Oh?"

"A few weeks more, I'll rob all the mammy-jammas
clean!"

"Wow!" I thought of a stream of exclamations, but
I could only analyze it while hearing it. I needed to
reflect, but your boy wouldn't allow it.

"But now, B., dig this! I pushed the Anyscape into
Rhythm Spectroscopic Transformation. And then I got
it tuned to combine the Anywhereness and the
Reappearance as music!"

"What? Brother, you know this is some deep
technical stuff."

"Aw, no it ain't. It's science. I can teach people how
to make and use these."

"What?"

"Now I added Rhythm Travel! You can disappear &
reappear wherever and whenever that music played."

"What?"

"So if you become "Black, Brown & Beige," you can reappear anywhere and anytime that plays."

"Go anywhere?"

"Yeh, like if I go into "Take this Hammer," I can appear wherever that is, was, and will be sung."

"Yeh, but be that song and you be on a plantation."

"I know." He was grinning. "I went to one." He was staring me down, winking without his eye. "I seen some brothers and sisters digging a well. They were singing this and I begin to echo. A big hollow echo, a sorta blue shattering echo. The Bloods got to smilin because it made them feel good, and that's the way they heard it anyway. But the overseers and plantation masters winced at that. They'd turn their heads sharply back and forth, looking behind them and at the slaves. Man, the stuff I seen!"

"You mean you been Rhythm Traveling already?"

"Yeh, I turned into some Sun Ra and hung out inside gravity. You probably heard of the Scatting Comet. Babs was into that."

"Really? Man, so—"

"I know. Why? What I'm gonna do with it? Yeh, but I'm just explaining now. I got a lotta tests."

"I guess so."

"But I want you to try it."

"Hey . . ."

"Hey, brother. Ain't no danger. Just don't pick a corny tune."

1995
(Originally published in Dark Matter, 2000)

Science & Liberalism

(A Short Tale)

"Like the time my man built this record player which took yr voice & played it back as music. But if you was lying, it would kill you.

"So we made him leave it at home when we went out.

"But then he pulled it out at the party.

"And everyone got outta there, one way or another.

"Naw, we wasn't there. Now they looking for him on TV!"

"Yeh," the other man said, "And you under arrest!"

1996

What Is Undug Will Be

The pretenders arrived after we'd found out they were pretenders, and the people killed them. Don't blame me with Sarah Vaughan, when we used to walk up the hill pointing at her house. It's the pretenders who make-believe her house ain't there no more, just a Boys & Girls Club the off pretend is for the on. I see that funny-looking sun and can't pretend it's the real one. The real one is locked up. You see, God is the guardian of Good, so it don't escape and get rid of bookkeeping. The missing front wheel—you can't have infinity without two good wheels. That's why the 1st Crazy Eddie was lame. See, the woman-headed lying nigger, so hip he could hang out in the desert forever waiting for a new horn, told the sister upstairs that the dude was really a human being. You know the riddle, hey diddle-diddle, niggers play second fiddle. Four legs, two legs, and three legs. But three legs is a lame. A FM who goes north becomes a MF. Frowny, he called himself, opening the supermarket of Dis. It was Hell, which was the future not coming. A two-legged man who never arrives. Then it was Hades. The past tense of wealth, which is insanity. Then dig, you knew where light went. You didn't understand that when you said "out" and the lame said "out," they was different outs. You wanted Bird to climb black fire wings wailing the blue raise of gone went. The square—I told him that was curtains—some snow juju greedy inside garbage that stunk with charm.

"To eat, you beat." Remember the slogan? What about, "Don't make me happy if you respect my intelligence." Remember that? The limping crazy motherfucker told us he discovered yodeling in a labyrinth—who else ate doo-doo while rich, squeezed Africa's titties for milk, stored in the refrigerator, waiting for Alan Ladd to kill him? And the withered bastard had a pen that shot poison swords. Remember Colonus? That's literary for frozen nigger pops, chocolate blood sweet. And the baseball mind—oh diamond crystal salt—which is white, ain't that right? He meant out as the city's enemy. We is in on all the time, except when we go out, like on out, which is where the good go and come to and from—is you with us, jitterbug? But out mean darkness which is hip, but lame mean that as if nothing could exist, it could. But wouldn't that be something? So now they come frowning and eating everything like the low cuss they call God. I told you a dog shit the church out of his backwardness. God is a broke short passing for in, but it's only out as in the opposite of off. And darkness, for a lame, has nothing to commend it but his cannibal breath and lying tongue. If you eat doo-doo your breath stink, or so the Pope do sing. And if feces ain't the past and turns into money, the cow jumps over the moon and never comes down, but frozen in the north, growing balls in the sky. And what is really ain't and what ain't is just a coat of paint and the devil own everything, and you see him on television, lame motherfucker.

That's why when the rest of on got hip to off and offed him, dug dis/stance was the graveyard, an illusion of skulls being on a flag—with you they background anonymous and still, except for the wind. And you know the Negro played God and the skull made-believe it had Malcolm behind them in white, a frame for the cross, which ain't even fishy—it's dead. What I say? And the skull tells the rest of the niggers to lay flat and passive like they worked in the museum, a tombstone for ideas which was a couple of weeks ago.

That's how long you been down, and I don't mean hip. Except at the top of your lying body is your woman, the only sane person in the desert, and you holding her back, being an animal and refusing to leave the ground, so it's a playground, now a desert, and it's the whole meal. Don't make me say it. You ain't got no more juice, except north, where they too hip to lie completely. Like half a lie is better than a full deck. Gravity. They in an airplane ruling. Or in a laboratory. They ain't Tarzan, and if they was, you warned them not to fall in the trap they set for you. So you joined Local 666 and they got you a gig in his movies as uncivilized. Dig that.

Pirates was not minerals, you found out (later), but they wanted to be. Brains was not edible (but they was) and spendable. So we changed the laws and slavery was actually a religion. Didn't your father dig it first and set himself up as invisible except for *De Toad* (Dutch for "murder victim")? Jesus! Yeh, him. With blond hair, and the deity Schwarzenegger, after you lost your warmth and came back looking like you had lost your skin to your limping kin.

Dude lost in a forest as a baby with a twin named Flawed Operator. Backwards, he wasn't no baby either. With Wolf Mama, the white blues singer. Janis, you dig? When it was us, she could see out both sides of the world, the past and the future. Now she's dead to confirm a lie, and a Dutch banker married her and sent her OD'd to paradise, which is an arrestable offense. Surround it. Don't let it sweeten the world. Don't let them be happy. Take the *p* out and give them a God that makes noise and flies, a woman that lives in Halloween with *Homo Locus Subsidere*, the bent-over junior Tarzan who bathes in toilets so he still think he bad. That mean bath. Remember Isabella, the transvestite Edgar Allan Poe of Middle America? Still pretending. That's why they get killed when now comes.

Stop getting High. This is what the initials told you. A message. The calendar's genius. Changed it. Julius and Augustus get in it, so with Paul that's 13, which is really unlucky. That mean dark, not like us, but like they mind which says when he stuck Cane in his eyes, it was to improve the Armed Forces. Especially the semen, which was dry since he left the best of it in his mama, then denied you was his one-drop overseas sun. Called you Moon, the Bob Marley of Ireland. That's where that mystery shit came in. Stonehenge. And the nigger nodding on the corner where you left him when you went to get fire, and where you dropped, everybody turned into new. Could sing like you. And dance. And was gone so long. Got so high, you forgot the you of I. And the time grew into a prison, the destination into a villain you looking for, and come was embarrassing if it was mentioned; go was half a vulgar job description.

I know the treble clef. From Thought, them Egyptians, your man who went further east. Your man. All them guys and dolls, I read about them niggers. Got outta here. When the band broke up and your arrival turned to stone and you couldn't understand yourself and started arguing with your own eyes. Like you could see what never will exist.

I remember your father told you your mother got here first. And you went with this karate muh-fuh. The blue was cool. The idea that there could be light, you couldn't dig. That was hard, since when we went up in the skyscraper and shit on the government, they thought they could turn to butter by circling our triple-hip outness, howling like they deserved to eat us.

But the Negro was run out of India. I saw a picture of him in the papers, blue. He went for it and made the lie a game, and the agony of the waiting room a country where money talked in consonants. A job. Remember when you was asking questions about that? Jesus! Come out the john, tricked by the Times. His accountant killed himself. His johnson betrayed him and told stories about his life that neglected to say he was impotent with fear. He was the 1st one at the tomb after the murder. Claimed the nigger had come back and told him that God wanted him at the Audubon, wanted him murdered to prove he could be the weatherman.

Got a job as a mystic in a candy factory, a private dick, hooked up with the scary quiet of delusion, a rock star, and made the big time before they hung him, ancient Mussolini style. Father Christmas was St. Nicholas of the normal. Like a white lie, which is like a circle around knowing. "Contain it," speaks the Yellow

Submarine, which is where your man went before they exposed him and put him on a cross to invent television and candy.

Stay out the mountains. That was a dumb statement. After the world broke up, there was a middle made of water. And your singing got large and you wanted to get in something and get away from your responsibilities as dead man—you was the Johnny Ray of being digested. You was Ahab later as an autobiography of your photograph, but disguised as Trane, high as the 1st father tripping out at the prison picnic.

Tender. The runner. The money. The soft of yourself before you was tricked. The pretender was your man, the goat lady, the ram of snot. Stay out the mountains. Here they come. Your boy was saying you a mulatto. Jacub, I knew him in his later years before he got to Chicago, when he was still building the mother ship, but he was so high it come out the father ship and could only fly to Rome. Your mama wasn't in it. He couldn't get no leg. That's why he called the sisters "nun." He wanted to be Elvis Presley once his man told him he could go north and start a newspaper for the little people. His gig had run out in other as jackleg—was this you or him? Oh, I see. When you took up singing, and he was copping your stuff as a shadow of the coming, which was cold when it went all the way out the way. The way they wanted out was north, not south.

That frown should have told you the city was not the town. They were in the future, like Dis, like Capital, like Hades when it was Havies. It's heavy. It's still Havies. Not you swimming with the woman. You the havie-not, the heavy knot on your past. The gas from your non-answerable prayer. An invisible invoice. You will not get paid.

Father Sex. You created Europeans from chains. You was Jacub before Hollywood. You created Hollywood because you didn't want to talk. You made the woman feline so you could teach philosophy while you was asleep.

So you created yourself as the answer to what you shouldn't have asked. It was perfect. Each drop of shit has something to say. Pray you ain't being talked about by what you create as waste. Haste, like we say, but tie up your camel and quit playing jazz. Use a rubber.

You ain't a pretender but sometimes I wonder why you pretend. You ain't the only mother that went, but you is the only father they sent. Your destiny has become an inverted design. Your future is smaller than Babel. So you be quiet and eat the questions as answers to your religion.

They killed the pretenders, I'm telling you. The animals who thought the world was endless feces. The runs. The races. Told you death was real, an advertisement for insect mercy-killing. Meditate while you head for the closet. Blue glass like your changed flick when they ran you out of contemplation with straight hair, the 1st cowboy.

Who could forget your lies about who was Mr. Hyde as you sped to that position as green thumb of the specific? I know you invented place so you could rest. That sign, the wave, as a picture of stopping. That tricked a lot of people. What about clef for the split in the stone? The G for the heaven, the top of your head where you thought light was a person, an owned creation necessary to go to your body, which you thought could be white stone.

Caste the first stone. Remember that? Dizzy with travel. Your songs stain your skin like the future candle of No. You censored us by leaving. Heard you was not the shepherd but the cow. You was not a woman but a number 3 on the hit parade, a ghost, which meant you wanted people to remember you when.

That's your brother, Sulumoor, whose mouth was always full of the wolf's tittie, whose milk ran through his veins, when Ali Baba was the future of his own past, where his skin had become trigonometry, and exile where he lived. A small piece of reality outside reality. So he was not the King of Is, and he couldn't take it. He had to get a job as a martial arts teacher and dreamt Ahab up to bolster the knock-out business. Looking at everybody crazy-eyed, called himself the night, love music, funk, storyteller. They called him Nunile and he left the sun home, but still he wanted to be known as Shine. Kicking people in the head for their own good. And when the writer showed, the end of the flow. Where the rain stopped and the bottom was the top and the top was the bottom and they were both opposite and the same and he was not normal—he had never been. His ease was now a thing to be described as grinning. He could be fertilizer for money.

You could be fertilizer for money. And you didn't understand. I told you that lame meant you no good and you left anyway, after you had kicked this Oriental in the face, talked about race so you could cop and not stop. You was sick, you know, like you found yourself, and you wouldn't correct yourself. You wouldn't read the proof of what was rite and write. And here the symbol magicians came and got your secrets as you left to go up in the mountains and become half-crazy.

Said you never was yourself, but you was. You wasn't your mother's son but her lover. Or was that you? No, you had changed, come out the mountains with a four-legged body and Abbey Lincoln's mind. But the rest of you was north and south and east and west, going to where they came from. Ignorant, they had been there as themselves before they became the self they didn't even know.

The fetish and the party, the maker and the doo-doo. You was talking about money and the goat you fucked. And here you come as your half-brother. Where was the sister, I asked. It wasn't just I, but I & I, but you was only half of you. And if you flew, you would a donut be. And when you copped, the middle dropped out of the world. You went—or was that the Arab?—the blessing of good, which is natural. Like your house high among the leaves, and your laughter, your face invisible to the animals. They was the ones who started that Mr. Hyde shit, so they could say they was doctors. They was jackals and looked up at your laughing ass, and sucked the bone of your solid waste and imitated your laughter and got on the hit parade and turned love into sex and revelation into a club, a balloon over a cartoon's head.

They learned the gibberish of your drunkenness and became the wizards, the old beings you left dead and bleached by not standing under the sun. The offed, the un-on. Laugh. They offered you a job as Othello, the distant greeting. A cry we thought was the fart of what does not exist. But you could get paid. The father of feeling? But that became religion. The entrance of the zoo became money. And charge was not the teaching of energy, but teeth.

You laughed so long your vision of prayer was walking away calling you dumb, because your droppings fertilized their resistance to being with you. They wanted to know why you wouldn't let them eat you, and you wouldn't tell them—couldn't tell them—because you was high, and began to lie that you was the closest thing to what you didn't understand, and started to say you was in charge, as well as out charge.

You wouldn't eat meat because it made you bad company, which was OK, but you couldn't hang with everybody because you made them mad by being where they couldn't see you, up in a tree laughing. And the doo-doo you dropped they copped and ate, and became warlike with starvation since you left their world and made them a church of getting and having, a heaven of menus, a fixed paradise where your self is the loser and the bank where they come out when they left. Your boy Remus was with them—oh, that's you, the werewolf. I dig. Where you is a delicacy. Brain food. And the mind is under the ground, where they left you. The south, where darkies laugh and beat on wood. And confuse happiness with morality.

And how and when did the pretenders get wasted? And who, be specific, was they? If you tend, you the on-maker (pardon me, officer), then you are the ever and the 1 added to 3—a 2 beat, New Orleans sound.

You hard to get along with because you know you

too well and don't understand your self. But I heard your music. I see you laughing like you was still in a tree. I seen you dancing one night. Your body, somebody said, was made of dark metal.

You are the animal stories, the descendant of the answer. Yeh, it is a trip, a question. Your mother is what is relevant, on forever, and where you go, Daddy-O, is where anything will be when it gets, changes my you into your me, or before it splits again. The boat rocking in rhythm near the dock, the blue waves like yourself upstairs, hiding inside your name.

I would have stopped us from killing the pretenders. But animals have no use for boats (except them ants who was trying to eat Charlton Heston, and that shit is understandable). But I was doing something else. And before I could say stop, they was gone. And the voice of me that would have saved them was gone before it even got here.

July 1996
Trancespoken by A.B. from the tongue of the X-rated "Bible"
Brick City, New Ark

Dream Comics

He was sitting on the porch scribbling on an envelope.

"What's happening, captain?"

"You mean, why am I sitting here scribbling and grinning?"

"Yeh, you ready to give out answers this early in the a.m.?"

"Yeh, listen to this!"

I put one foot on the bottom step of the little orange wooden porch. There were only three steps. The house: an old, wooden, orange, whipped-looking one-family house. Well, not quite a one-family house—maybe a half-family house. My man was grinning even wilder now.

"Hey, what's with you? You saw the one-armed man who killed Richard Kemble's wife on TV singing Sam & Dave's greatest hits?"

"Yeh, wasn't that a trip? I mean, he can walk around without getting arrested, and even run for public office."

"So that's why you smiling?"

"No, funnier than that. Just before I went to sleep I came to understand that *Tarzan* and *Schwarzenegger* got the same meaning."

"What?"

"Yeh, they both mean *black-black*. Like black-squared." This cracked him up. "Yeh, like double-black. Super black. Dig it . . . *Tar*, from *Ptah*, the 1st ancestor, which means black. And *Zan*, from *Zanj*, also meaning black."

"Huh?"

"And *Schwarz*, which also means black. And I know you know what *Negger* means, however they want to mess around with it. Yeh, Negger. Us in the funny papers. See, black-black, double-black, super black, black to the second power." He cracked up again.

It broke me up too. "Yeh, wow—"

"Hey, did you know the word *wow* is an ancient black war cry? It went all the way into the British Isles—Ireland, Scotland, Wales. There was Bloods up there too. Man, these people always . . . But that black-black business. You see they need a white Negro, like Norman Mailer said. Remember that, Mailer's hype back in the '50s? *The White Negro*. So they got one. You know, like Paul Muni or Paul Newman on the chain gang. Travolta getting down like he one of the Copasetics. Then he came back a hip angel. Shit."

"Yeh, I see what you're saying. That's wild. That'll make you smile alright, even laugh straight out, if it wasn't for all the papal bull that go with that."

"Hmm . . ." He looked distracted from a moment. "Yeh, that's something. A bull. The Pope, John Bull, bull market, bullshit—the most precise. Picasso's monster bull in that labyrinth with that weird lantern. Then all them fools in Spain running them bulls every year. Isabella got the Inquisition coming in—they better run."

I was full up laughing so hard at the very thought of how this brother gets into this stuff. Words are one of his things. He's always breaking shit on you. Like he told me, jazz is really *jism* or *jasm*. Like it's *come music*. Or *On* was the name of a city in Africa where the Bloods kept track of the sun. *Turn On*, dig?

"Hey, man. You a funny dude."

He looked up from his bull thoughts. "What?"

"That's why you was smiling?"

"No, no. Well that too, but something even funnier."

"You got more? Well give it up."

"I had a dream last night about Mick Jagger."

"Mick Jagger! That corny, no-dancing, no-singing motherfucker?"

"That's right. First time I ever had a dream about Mick Jagger."

"I hope so. Mick Jagger. Man, you wasting your dream space on that clown. What was it about?"

"I dreamed Mick Jagger stopped me in a bar—"

"A bar? Man, you don't even drink. Since when you hanging out in bars?"

"Hey, man, don't interrupt. That is weird though, ain't it? But anyway, I was in this bar and Mick Jagger comes up to me and starts talking shit about how great he is. And how the Rolling Stones was the greatest rock and roll band in the world."

"Damn, what kinda shit is that? Man, you musta had some all-the-way-out shit to eat before you went to bed."

"Naw, naw. I don't eat nothing before I go to bed."

"OK, OK. So what happened?"

"Well, he come up to me talking shit and it pissed me off. So I killed him! Killed him dead. And left him there in the bar with drunk people pointing at him, wondering if they should call the police. That's why I was smiling. That's why I was scribbling too, so I could remember the dream."

"What? Jesus Christ! You all the way out, partner." And we both started to laugh so hard we doubled over.

"But look at this." He shoved the *Star-Liar* at me. The headline read, *Corny-Ass Mick Jagger Gets Wasted*.

Yeh, it was true. No, not right now. This was my man's future laughter. That newspaper ain't out yet either.

February 1997

A Letter

I didn't want to see it or hear it but wanted it. Things are themselves, & like us, resist being anything else. Ready or not, can you imagine hearing that from a parking meter?

Who are you? the cars asked, but I ignored them. I sd it's raining, but didn't speak so the shop windows smirked.

They refused to carry my reflection. So what? Miles Davis fed that through my inner ear. The streetlights explained, *Hard Edge*. The Museum left its names tapping on the bldgs to remind me of dead friends.

I don't believe in ghosts. Because they don't believe in themselves. That's why they don't exist. Suppose you were so fixed on the dirt you cdnt get away when the box car visibled.

When I turned the corner, there were two more. I smiled as if I was going to acknowledge them. Ha. So that's what that murmur *Fat chance!* meant. It was a billboard being nasty. Like a beggar w/credit cards. The thought pissed me off. I stopped & stared at the dumb camel. The poison gadget in its mouth.

Bill Cosby lived around the corner. A marquee was spitting up. It looked like sparks to the lovers trailing me with one eye.

OK, OK, I'll do it, I thought. There was no need to tell my Self I didn't know what I was thinking about.

A car skidded. Two robbers ran by trying to get their masks off before they were shot. They tossed me their gun. That's why I'm writing from jail.

Yours,
Lefty

1998

Conrad Loomis & the Clothes Ray

L oomis was an old friend of mine. I kept in touch with him more or less regularly, but every few months he would vanish, so to speak. At first, I thought he would hide out when he hit the picket. He did do that a couple of times. He'd hit the number, get the cash, and then get away from everybody and spend it all. We used to tease him about this. And he hit a few times. But that's because he'd spend so much money on that stuff. He might spend a hundred dollars a week trying to hit the picket. So when he did, he was still in the red, because he spent so much all the time.

Conrad was also a chemist—at least he was in college. But I thought he'd flunked out of chemistry. He said that didn't stop him from learning the heavy stuff. He flunked the light stuff because it was boring. That sounded like an *Esquire* magazine article on Einstein, you know? So I just nodded, though I did think it was probably true, at least in Conrad's head.

He had some chemistry-type jobs, paint factories, the mad Delaware Nazis who run DuPont. That kind of stuff. But eventually he would always get bounced for some reason. No, it wasn't "some" reason. It was very specific. Conrad would always be trying to do his own thing during company time. You know that don't get over. Neither did Conrad.

Well, he called me up one night about 2 in the morning and said he hated to disturb me, but he had something which could get us both rich if I came over immediately. If I didn't come over immediately, then he would know that I wasn't really serious and he would get somebody else.

See, that's the kind of trick people put you in. It wasn't the money, but I didn't want to seem like I wasn't interested in Conrad's ultimate concern. But damn, "It's 2 o'clock, Conrad. Why didn't you call me earlier?"

"I hadn't finished. You coming or not?"

See, that's the same kind of stuff people pull on you. "Coming or not? Damn, man. What about tomorrow?"

"Oh, I see. You jiving. That's the trouble with Negroes. They ain't serious about nothing."

"Man, why you call me up in the middle of the f'n night with some tired shit like that? Please, Negro."

"Hey, I just thought that you was serious. Shit, I even thought you was my friend. But—"

"OK, OK." See, that's the kind of stuff people pull. "OK, I'll come over there. But just don't be jiving yourself. Dig? Man call me up in the middle of the night. You think cause you up in the middle of the night, you serious?" But he'd already hung up the phone.

Now what I'm about to tell you has been in the papers, but in a very small type and then not the whole story. Actually, all these things are still going on, the whole garbage. Conrad had done something fantastic, but he didn't really know how to handle it. He asked me for my opinion, and I gave it to him. I don't know if I was right or wrong. Conrad disagreed with me and did what he wanted and got busted, or not really busted, but hunted, sort of. Like Salman Rushdie or somebody. But see, that don't mean what I told him was correct either.

Conrad's sitting in the middle of the floor when I come in his spot. He's resting and the door of the joint was open. Yeh, he's asleep in the middle of the floor and got this hair dryer (or that's what it looked like to me) resting on his stomach, like he'd just fell out or something.

"Oh, this mammy-jammy drunk," I was whispering to myself, when he opened his eyes one at a time. He immediately leaped up from the floor, jumping around me like Mick Jagger. At least that's what I told him—we both hate Mick Jagger, the no-dancing, no-singing . . .

"Hey, man. Don't bring up no swine like Mick Jagger on me. I got something. Yes, indeed. And it's perfect that you, my main man, should be on hand to dig it. We both gonna get entirely fantastically awesomely rich."

"Yeh, yeh." See, Conrad has made this statement to me a bunch of times before. What's a bunch? Well, maybe fifty times in the last five years. One time we did get some chump change off a number, but we hadn't made no money off his work. First, because he wouldn't show nobody nothin'—he'd only make vague references to his "work." For a lot of people, that became a joke. "Conrad's work" became a synonym in our crowd for anything you didn't know which was taking up somebody's time.

"Oh, so now you gonna run out 'your work' for me, on the real side? Or is this just another coming attraction?"

"Look, man. You should be glad you're intelligent. Ha ha ha." He broke into that little whiny laugh of his, like radio static organized by mirth. Is that abstract?

"What's so funny?"

"Well, that's it. Really, that's it."

"What's it?"

"Intelligent! See, you're intelligent. No shit. You're a very intelligent brother. But see, I'm outtelligent." He laughs, ditto as before.

"Outtelligent? Yeh, you seem that way to me. You make up that word?"

"Yeh, I made it up. But it existed always since it was in the world, scrambled up in the letters. Plus, I'm sure some other outtelligences dug themselves long before me."

"Outtelligent? What's the difference between . . . Oh, I know. Intelligent deals with the in stuff. Outtelligent deals with the out stuff."

"Exactly, I knew you'd understand." He laughs again. "But see, just like that, understand? Most people can just understand. But I can over and understand at the same time."

Conrad talked like this all the time. It was cool until you became hungry or wanted to dig another scene. And when that idea came to your mind, he'd say almost perfunctorily, *See ya later!* And you'd split.

"OK, brother. Over, under, out instead of in, but what you get me here for? God knows I know you outtelligent and overstanding, but what's up?"

"OK, now look at me."

"I am looking at you. I been looking at you. So what?"

"What do I have on? Describe my clothes."

Conrad was about five-feet-eight or -nine, but he'd sometimes add a few inches depending on who he was talking to. I remember he told some sister he was six feet tall and she said she believed him. I never believed she did though.

But how was he dressed? He was usually in a black sweater and black pants with a black whatever on top. He always looked like he was in something. Like some organized whatever. He never was, to my knowledge. But dig, he was not in the black outfit tonight. "What color is that stuff?"

He had on . . . I don't know what he had on. It was the same kind of stuff, I guess. He still looked like he was in something. But the stuff was expensive-looking. It had a darkness to it. It was black, but had a blue sheen coming out from under it, like . . . I dunno. "What is that?"

"I designed all of this." He wheeled around to let me see. He was sort of snorting inside that outtelligent laugh. "It's out, ain't it?"

"Yeh, it's out. What is it?"

"My clothes. Mine."

"Yeh, but what kind of cloth is it?" It did glow. I reached to touch it and felt a bizarre thing. I felt his skin. When I ran my hand up his arm it felt like he didn't really have anything on, like it was his bare skin. "What in the hell kind of stuff is that? It feels like—"

"Like I don't have anything on!" And this cracked him up. He kept wheeling around laughing. "Yeh, that's it. That's it. That's an intelligent observation. But wait till I hip you. This is some outtelligent jammy, my man, very outtelligent."

"Yeh, I can dig that." It was strange. I touched it again. Like his skin, for real, like he had nothing on. "What is it, Conrad? Will you let me in on the stuff, since you brought me all the way over here?"

"I don't have anything on!" He laughed some more. "You're right, I don't have anything on at all. And because of this, I don't have to wash them. I don't even have to change them if I don't want to." And he kept laughing.

"What are you talking about? You don't have nothing on?" I felt again. That's what it felt like. "Well, will you tell me what the hell you're doing?"

That's when he hoisted this little hair dryer–looking thing in my face. "See this? This is the Clothes Ray. I invented it. I made it up in my mind a long time ago, but it didn't seem really important until a few months ago when I didn't have nothing to wear." Some more laughter.

"OK, OK." He shoved the dryer in my hand. Actually, it looked like some kind of lantern. Like a stage light, a Fresnel or something. "So what's this do?"

"I told you, it's my Clothes Ray. You just turn it on, and bang-o."

"Bang-o, what?"

"Bang-o. You get the kind of clothes you thinking about, whatever you can make up. You can't wear no stuff people are already wearing—that's just technology. This is deeper than that. You see, I can make clothes by altering the light, rearranging the light faster, slower, different wavelengths, angles, different kinds of motion to the rays."

"Yeh?" I didn't know what he was talking about.

"Dig. Everything is, to some degree, a form of light. It's matter in motion—you know that. But it is, in essence, different forms and degrees of illumination."

"Yeh, yeh." What was he saying?

"So I can rearrange the light, and by doing this, recreate it as anything else it has the focus to become. The focus has to be supplied by the creator, the designer."

"Designer? You mean you make clothes out of light?"

"Now you coming." He laughs. "Yeh, now you coming. Yeh, I can make clothes, any kind of clothes out of light, with my Clothes Ray here."

"What?"

"You wanna see? Take off your clothes—that's the best way. I could put some duds on you over those sorry vines you got on, but naked is better, fits better."

"No, I ain't taking my off my clothes. Just do it."

"OK, you gonna be hot and sweaty. But dig."

Now he switched on this light. There was some kind of negligible hum, a flashing, and something sounding like voices coming from inside the thing. "What's that?"

"Oh, that's me speaking to the machine from inside it. I put a CD inside that activates the light transformation by sound. I can alter it if I change my basic design. What kind of clothes you want?"

"Anything?"

"Yeh, but not something somebody already got."

"Why not? That stuff you got on looks like something somebody else got."

"Yeh, but it ain't. Look at this, brother. Shit, you don't know what you talking about."

The form of the clothes—what looked like a simple sweater, shirt, and pants—did look common, but they had that glow I talked about. Like it was made of television.

"OK, I want a leather coat like no leather coat nobody ever had."

"OK, you want an unleather coat. Dig."

He adjusted the "dryer," turned some dials, and my whole body lit up on the outside like a neon sign. And gradually, and not a long time either, I sort of grew a coat around me. It felt like it had the body of leather—the feel—but it was much lighter and I could not really feel a weight to it at all. There was a kind of warmth to it, like when you touch a bulb, but not that hot. But it was something that was on.

"Is this real, or just some kind of illusion?"

"Well, everything is real that exists. But at the same time, since it's in constant motion, turning and twisting, rising and changing, there is a quality of illusion to it. But now, the clothes are not illusory. They exist, except they're made—"

"Of light! Yeh."

Conrad started to laugh and dig his handiwork on me, hopping around to check the coat out. It was a leather-looking coat, but you knew at once it wasn't leather. It was lit up from the inside and fit perfectly, or would have if I had taken off my other clothes.

"Aha, now you want to know everything. Yeh, I dig now."

"Yeh, I want to know everything, but the first thing I want to know is—"

"What I'm gonna do with it?"

"Yeh, what you gonna do with it?" The idea of making clothes for people in some kind of place was obvious. The wealth that could be made—that was also pretty obvious. But there was a monkey in this, a chimpanzee crawling around us shouting stupid things, things that were nevertheless true. A signifying cross-dialogue of us to ourselves, without speaking. Except, "You know, Conrad, everybody ain't gonna be thrilled with this."

"What you mean, won't be thrilled with it?"

"You ever see a picture called *The Man in the White Suit*?"

"Of course. Well, I never saw it, but I read what it was about. Actually, that's what gave me the idea. But that was a long time ago."

"Well, if you had seen the flick, you know that the people who make clothes tried to kill Alec Guinness. They tried to steal his invention, because like yours, it would put them out of business."

"Oh yeh. I read that. You see Mamet's *The Water Engine*?"

"You a Mamet fan?"

"Oh, man. It was on television. But it was OK, shit. That told me what you talking about."

"How you mean?"

"Well, in the Mamet thing, a guy invented an engine that ran on water and they killed him and took it."

They way he said all this should have given me confidence—that he did know what he was getting into—but somehow it didn't, because he seemed to think that he could not be stopped by mere intelligence, since he was "outtelligent." And that sent a cool razor up my back. I didn't think of any foul play or anything, but . . .

"How they gonna bother me? I told you—"

"I know, you outtelligent. But dig, Mr. Out T., is you bulletproof?"

Conrad laughed and cut it off quick like a shot. "Shit, I can be. That ain't no big thing. I could figure that shit out in a hot minute."

"Oh, for Christ's sake, Conrad! Rich people, Upper East Side. They won't let you up there, even if they didn't know the shit you putting down. And if some of those people find out, especially here in New York—the Garment District, remember?—then your ass will really be up against it."

He was listening, but like how you listen to somebody out of politeness who really doesn't know what they're talking about.

"Yeh, you don't believe me. But what about finding some sympathetic organization or country—a Third World country? Best would be a Socialist country like Cuba, North Korea, or even China, despite that the clown running it used to wear a dunce hat."

"What? No, nobody else. Me and you. We'll do it for a couple of years, then vanish. That's all. Move around the world, make billions. Watch."

"It's a great invention, brother. But listen to me, these whatnots will not let you make no billions. They against they own folks other than them making billions. Don't you know that? It ain't really about race—it's about money."

"Yeh, I know that. That's why I know we can get over. Money talks."

"Yeh, money kills too. For money."

"Ah . . ." He waved me off.

"Yeh, remember that brother who was supposed to be the richest Blood in the world? Smith? He supposed to have died suddenly of an aneurism. But then they tried to put out that he got cancer from a cellular phone. They had set fire to his house a few months before. The guy that owned the orange juice company. I don't believe none of that stuff. In fact, I called his daughter and asked her what she thought, and she got pissed off and slammed down the phone."

"I ain't him."

"He ain't him neither, no more."

This set Conrad to laughing. "You gonna help me or not?"

"OK, OK. But we got to move cautiously on this, brother. Not that I don't want to make the big bucks, but I know, and I thought that you did too."

"Know what?"

"I thought you knew where you were, who you were dealing with."

1998

The Used Saver

The Regulator of Usury arrived at his pied-à-terre in Washington just forty minutes after leaving the Fed. He took off all his clothes immediately w/o looking around as he turned on no lights going into the bedroom.

The light seemed like it took too long to come on. He blinked as if making a sound, but continued until he stood w/shorts & socks. All his clothes piled on the bed.

Eppsmith was still single at fifty-five, never even a "catch" to the circle he measured life by. Not ugly, there was no proof. He could not be seen except if you opened yr wallet. And there he sat, "Federal Promissory Note" his handle. When appeared otherwise, if he did not speak, there was an absence. If you took a photograph, expensive cameras wd reflect a green glow where he shd have been.

He was part of money. In correctness & crisp white & greenness. He was presidential, a brown king even as a baby, an Irish chief, a biblical Jewish patriarch. Not actually, but it amused him to glamorize his blankness. He wd use evening dreams like this to see himself as he wd be, if he actually cd be detected. Farrakhan sd at the MMM that he cd see Eppsmith. He called him 19 and I was told it meant a youthful negative. Little No. We didn't understand, but he was dropping it.

Eppsmith was visible when paper money was

displayed. The more displayed, the more he haunted the place, observable till passed. If you spread money all over yr place, you cd hear him like the robbers who had to tip up on the private dick and were foiled.

Eppsmith didn't think about money all the time. He thought about numbers & credit more. He was the Chief Explainer of the National Debt. He knew the magic that Moses used to dis the Egyptian magicians. He was proof that the Red Sea cd be parted if you had connections.

He was not religious, so to name any religion as "his" wd make you funny to him. He wd not deny the religious label—he wd be sourly gratified to confirm yet another fool. His self-evaluation soared with fools, but more importantly, he knew the game was not yet secure. No one generally knew where the rabbit came from or where it went. "To be anything except a counter—a Knower, a figure of evocative power."

Eppsmith opened the bathroom door and a young black man with a Chinese machine pistol was taking a shit on the commode. He heard it drop, the splash hitting the blue water.

The black guy just looked up and nodded, the pistol loosely across his knees as he did Number One, reading *What is to be Done?* by V. Lenin, the Peking edition.

Eppsmith backed up inadvertently. Nothing came out of him; there was no money displayed, so the shitter thought it was his own reflection whipping off the mirror.

But he called out, "Eppsmith, you evil bastard! I'll get a dollar—no, a ten!—a federal note, yr funny money, so you can show up & I can ask you something."

E. turned now & the young man came out of the

john pulling his pants up & tossing ten dollars on the floor. Eppsmith had no legs. He appeared to the waist, so he couldn't move.

"Eppsmith, listen! What is the meaning of money? Explain credit! Explain the national debt!" The young shitting man pointed his weapon at the part of Eppsmith he could see.

"Why are you doing crazy things? You'll be killed even if you mean no harm."

"Explain, that's all!"

Back in the bathroom, another person, a white man with his overalls hanging at his sides, began to take a crap. He was reading a book called *The National Question*.

Another man sat on the sink. He had a newspaper. There was a picture of Eppsmith chained to a safe with banknotes stuffed in his mouth. People were laughing.

"Ignorant assholes!" Eppsmith screamed. "Ignorant lowlife assholes!" Now Eppsmith had passed indignant, which he thought was brave.

But one shitter reached into his pocket and threw Eppsmith's legs onto the floor. So E. walked fast away, still carrying his clothes, looking for an overcoat. He was leaving. Where were the keys? If he cd . . .

"Eppsmith, forget those questions for a minute. Do you understand usury and why all the religions banned it? Why Jesus threw the money-lenders out of the temple?"

"Yes. My family came to America. We were Red Babies. Rothschilds. I was born as the bank note was legal. I am the note." He laughed. "The idea is all it is, you know."

"It's paper," the white boy said. "You are invisible w/o it, but where are you when you can't be seen?"

E. turned and stalked into the kitchen. He had a robe. He had a gun up the stairs. The Negro moved, but not sharply. He called, "Eppsmith! Usury—what is it, for real?"

Eppsmith in the kitchen broke into a meeting of Puerto Ricans—it looked like blacks & West Indian blacks. A white foolish teacher-looking person drinking orange juice in nervous gulps.

A black woman at the table sd, "Eppsmith, you're going on the tube in a half hour to explain usury."

"What?" Eppsmith was seething. "Is this foolishness—this break-in & entering—yr idea? The police are across the hall!"

"No," the woman sd. "The police are in the dumbwaiter beating a Negro by mistake. He loves the police."

A person walked into the room picking up the notes & Eppsmith flew into a wedge of space that a moth unknowingly circled. His heart was a memory of neon bells. He sulked at his advantage. He could disappear. He could not laugh though. He was invisible by law & there were rules governing one's acts.

"Eppsmith, he's here, right?" A big Indian, a red-brown Cherokee-looking dude. The others pointed at E. He didn't understand how they cd be so accurate.

"Usury, Eppsmith. You're going on TV to explain it. And the national debt."

Eppsmith was pouting, but a large check wd do it—a credit card. His eyes were vexed when he cd be dug.

"No, that religious language has been long obsolete!"

One of the group began to chain him, though he

was not hurt when it was all over. Shaken very badly, but he carried a Derringer in his wallet. It was an advertising campaign. The intruders used his photo & asked those questions in red on posters which soon flooded the city.

It was serious, Eppsmith realized, when more & more people began to ask him the same questions. *What is the nature of money? What is usury? What is credit? What is the national debt?*

He had an appointment this afternoon to discuss it. What was to be done? Eppsmith was stunned, amazed. There he was, answering, explaining clearly the private control of America's money, the robbery of public monies used to secure & seize new markets for the corporations. What was wild was E. kept fidgeting & returning, so it seemed he was a sinister demon or wizard explaining how private banks got control of America's money. How they print & sell you your money because they own it & only give you what they can steal.

In two weeks, the entire episode was suddenly appearing on national television. *Like a computer virus*, the authorities explained. E. now had a bodyguard, a one-armed Kansan, but very efficient. He had met him before in Chicago, at the Kemble's party.

People are so ugly, Epp thought, wincing at his bodyguard's fascinating life. He had run for president, and when he lost, people started saying they recognized him as the one-armed man who really murdered Kemble's wife.

He & Epp talked for hours every day. They were advised to stay inside until the videotape stopped appearing. By that time, they would also have destroyed all copies of *The Fugitive* as well.

1998

My Man Came by the Crib the Other Day . . .

(For Grachan)

You know the dude I told you about before, the Rhythm Travel brother?

Yeh, yeh, I know.

But dig this, he come up with some really *other* stuff this time.

Other stuff? Shit, I thought that Rhythm Travel was all the way other. Man, what could be more other than that? Plus, I thought he fixed it so you cdnt remember nothing when you left.

I thought I was gonna be slick and asked him could I tape the shit so I could remember.

He let you do that?

No. Dude so out, he wrote down the formula for the stuff and said if I was really out, not half-out or heard about out, or rich, I could figure it out myself.

Yeh? And you figured it out?

Well, almost. What I did was figure out what I got to figure out.

Aw, man. You shucking.

No, dig this. I wrote out what I got to find out to find out how he do this shit!

Oh yeh? Well . . .

I see you ain't trying to figure out shit.

Naw, I'ma let y'all be the *Outs*, and I'ma be the *In* that dig the out.

Yeh, dig that jive. Anyway, if you look at this first symbol . . .

Yeh, what is it?

Damn, can't you see? It's a bird . . .

It's a plane . . .

I dunno why I'm wasting my time trying to hip you to some shit all the way beyond yr ass.

Probably because yr man feel the same about you.

Yeh, right. But dig, that's a bird, right?

I know, the Egyptian hieroglyphic for Soul, BA, the human-headed soul.

Yeh, so you ain't altogether, Clarence.

Man, why you wanna call me yr boy's name? You think I'm a Wooden Negro like him?

Well, y'all do resemble each other around the pockets.

Why you diverting the conversation, brother? Yr shit must be shaky.

OK, Bird, BA, Soul, Phoenix, Tail or Tale on Fire. Rise out of Fire every 100 years. Actually taken from Fetish, where the lower Nile northerners got the spirit paradigm from the upper Nile southerners.

Man, I know that. You think you Dr. Ben?

No, I'm Dr. Is . . .

I told you, you shd be a standup comedian so you can pay for yr fone bill.

But the point I'm making . . . The bird is an IBIS, which means—

What?

See, you don't know, do you?

I Be I Is . . .

What the *weise knabe* call Stork.

Stork all them motherfuckas. Including Bomba Bill and his new instrument, the Monica.

I heard that from you last time. One of them Low Coups.

President Clinton's in a bad position/Not as President/But as a musician./His critics say, if you listen to them,/Bill wasn't playing nothing./He got his Monica/Blowin him.

Wow, that's truly corny.

I got it from you.

That don't make it not corny. Just familiar . . .

Hey, brother. Are you gonna tell me the stuff about the outer than out?

Bird, next, eye, RA, 9, are am, next snake, wisdom, Blood landlord in Eden drove yr kinfolks out the garden.

My kinfolks? See, I hate a prejudiced motherfucker.

Man, will you go on with yr recitation without this suspicious hesitation?

Oh, now you gon get into my shit.

Hey, brother. Remember, I taught you everything you know.

Yeh, then you included in the demand for reparations. Wondered I didn't know shit.

See, you admit it.

See, it's very hard to tell an ignorant motherfucka anything.

That's right, I been trying to get you to understand that for years.

Aw, man. Don't square up on me just like the rest of the Melicans. Either tell me the other or get further.

Yeh, I remember that. *And smell better.* Anyway, dig . . . You ain't gonna believe it, cause yr reparations claim is absolutely correct.

Listen, dig this. (Bends slightly as if to whisper.) This motherfucka done found a way to regrow yr teeth.

Aw, man. Come on. These folks ain't even been able to grow hair, no matter what the Totally Vile keep lying about. What kinda shit you talking about? Growing teeth . . . Damn. What, you high? And if you is, where mine, greedy bastard?

See, that's yr problem. I ain't sd nothing about *these folks.* I'm talking about my man, Sun Tan.

Sun Tan. I thought his name was—

You thought you farted but you shit. I ain't never told you his name.

Why not?

Security reasons.

Security? From who?

Who you think? The Lord of the Flies. The Beast who rose smoking from the Western Sea. Gog's brother, the other Other, who actually fucked his mother, killed his father, and put out his own eyes in the name of modernism.

Oh, yr boy, Dicht.

Yeh, and the whole Tator family, including Santa Claus and Christy Whitman.

OK, OK. I believe anything after watching the Vikings sell them playoffs like that. Told you about having a worm in yr sperm.

Look, bro. Anybody—not just some little Blood, so black he blue—could get invisible, rob banks for scientific research, use music to travel.

I know them airlines don't like *that* shit.

Plus some other Other shit I can't talk about, it's so out.

I know, plus you can't remember.

Yeh, dig this. This dude can make clothes from light!

Whaaaaat?

He got a machine that if you lie when he got it on, it'll take you OUT! This dude—

Hey, man. Fuck that shit. Don't tell me no other shit. I don't want the Beast or one of his experimental body slaves beatin at my door.

Ha, you mean like yr boy, *Homo Locus Subsidere* ("Near Man").

Yeh, or yr boy, whose name in the ancient texts means, *Odor Eats.*

Hey, I meant to ask you . . . why yo boy HLS—Near Man, right—wow, why he got a white ring around his mouth?

That's an award, brother. Brecht called it the *Caucasian Chalk Circle.* It's given to Courageous Coons who have, by their display of Extreme Negrossity, been inducted into the Loyal Order of Proven Condoms who act as Dicht's Tung, thereby confirming how even Coons can make Herr Penis mightier than we sawed.

What?

Right, hence the CCC lips as a sort of a service ribbon, to indicate the bearer has received the Golden Kneepads, which are only to be worn at Secret Special Gatherings of the Knee Cult.

The Knee Cult?

I gave you that paper where this sister—she's a

detective—was commissioned by the Self-Determination Council, and reported actually witnessing one of the rituals.

Yeh, I remember. The Knee Cult Surveillance. Wow, now that was wild. I thought that was fiction.

That don't stop it from being Real, you dig?

OK, but growing teeth, regrowing teeth? In old people? In anybody? Shit, he could grow teeth on a chair if he wanted to.

Yeh, but why would you need teeth on a chair?

Aw, man. Bump you.

Well, if he can grow teeth, re-grow teeth, even in old people, how come nobody don't know about it? How come it ain't famous?

Why you think I'm telling *you*?

Hey, man. Where you going? You ain't told me nothing yet about the stuff.

I'm sorry, brother. You took up too much of my time. I gotta get to my man, Grachan, before he go to the dentist!

1999

A Monk Story

I was at Monk's funeral with Amina. But then a few months later, I run into him in Newark!

I stopped dead in my tracks. I could feel the October wind filling my mouth.

"Monk" slowed to look at me. He started smiling, sort of, when I froze.

"You think I'm . . ." was his 1st words.

"Uh, yeh. Wow . . ." was what I managed. I knew it couldn't be him. But believe my eyes, it was him!

"Monk" allowed that deep throat laugh, which convinced me more it was him.

"But you was at that guy's funeral. I heard your mouth back there criticizing the Jazz Preacher."

"Naw. But man, whoever you are, you look—"

"Yeh, I know. Hey, what can I do? But this is me anyway, not that dead guy."

The man could be Monk, really. There was nothing I could pin that wasn't. The face, the size, the walk, the blue nearly wrinkled vine, the stingy brim sky pressing his ears.

"Monk" had a ring he twisted on his finger to check. It made him do a sudden slick-step. A preface to his eyes resettling into my face like the brush of notes vibrating my skin.

"What's yr name, brother?" I was recovered from

the shock. I knew it wasn't Monk, but this dude was an incredible replica.

"Monk!" He had a ragged line to his mouth, trying not to laugh. But Monk always looked like that.

"Monk?" Laughing, laughing like we do. It was funny alright, but the man wasn't smiling anymore. Oh, maybe he was. But his mouth was stretching into scatting "Jackieing," that hip number. Listening took me away from the mystery, but I'd by then agreed in my answer. A Monk digger who looked like the High Priest.

For a couple minutes, the two of us, at the corner of Branford Place and Halsey Street, stood there dipping and learning some of Monk's steps. It was a groove because the dude scatted like a horn.

No, he was scatting like a box! A piano! No, I mean in my ear, head, I heard a piano. I heard Monk out of this dude's mouth!

"But what's yr name, man? Is it really Monk?"

"What you mean?" He shot that stare reserved for Squares.

"Alright, yr name is Monk. But you ain't saying—" It sounded stupider to me than it does now.

"Hey, man. I ain't never been dead! I wasn't in that jive box they had in the church. Plus, Monk lived in the city. I'm from home."

"From home? The South?"

"Yeh." He lit up around the eyes, but his mouth broke into a narrow rest. "The South Ward."

"You from Newark?"

"I ain't from Newark, I'm *in* there! You see me. It ain't a *from*."

I was laughing, but my afternoon was bent in a hip way. The top of my head was warm, like when you want to tell somebody right away. "You been in Newark? How old are you?"

"Hey, man, I don't tell my age."

"No?"

"No. You should stop telling yours too. People start to believe you believe in time!"

Now the laughing was filling up my whole head. There was a kind of delight in it. Not the "mystery," because I thought I'd already floated into that rationality. But the feeling there were millions of hip people on the planet. That we public hipsters were only the tip of that top. The number was out there and rising. The I's of the Eyes who knows and hears. Who dig the sounds. Who can understand this Dis and the Cover. Who love the classics, the masters, the ultimate live beauty of "the music."

"Wow, this is really deep. I mean, you are Monk. I mean, really . . . I mean, not just the way you look and sound, but—"

"Yeh, I told you my name. And you trying to hook me up with the dead brother. You can see I ain't dead."

"Yeh, yeh." More laughter. "I know." Like that, you might say anything. So I say, "You don't . . ."

"Go on."

"You don't play piano, do you?"

"What you mean, do I? If I was gonna be named Monk, wouldn't I play the piano?"

"Well, you could be a wide receiver for the Jets."

Like he hadn't replied, he said, "That's another Art!"

Man, that was funny. "He ain't your first cousin, that Art?"

"I don't know if he 1st. But he close. Only a couple more catches."

More fun, football getting in like that.

"But—" I started.

"No, let's get it straight. You don't believe in no ghosts and shit, do you?"

"Naw, man."

"Then the only answer is I'm another Thelonious."

"Is that yr 1st name?" Please! This dude was taking me over Niagara without a barrel.

"Yeh, Thelonious Sphere Monk."

"Hey, brother." I was trying to make conversation really. But I guess that cold analytical tip must've poked out. The dude half-laughed and half-humphed to get me to check myself. "OK." I apologized for being lame. "It's just the whole thing is out—really out."

Suddenly, the man turned to look at the traffic. A black Rolls was easing toward the curb. An old white woman in a maroon turban was sticking her head out the window, as if looking for someone. "Monk" stepped back into a storefront entrance and gestured at me to follow. It was amazing. I caught a look at the woman, who was scanning the street impatiently. No, no. It hit me. That woman looks like . . .

"It's the Baroness." "Monk" was half-whispering and half-snorting.

"The Baroness?" It was not possible. But it was her. Rica. The wealthy groupie in whose apartment Bird died and where the other(?) Monk occasionally hung out. The woman in fact was, despite the hype, not a favorite of a lot of people who saw her as an Anne Rice character created specially to suck jazz masters' blood.

"You mean you know the Baroness too?"

"Aw, man. Why don't you stop that double-doubting denial and dig reality? I'm not dead, Rica's not dead."

He was doing one of his steps to some scat in his head. "I'm ducking her!" Monk was back in the doorway grooving now.

"When that other dude died and they treated Nellie like that, reading Rica's shit in the church—that shit drugged me. That's why I'm ducking her. And will be." He stared at me like conversation.

2000

Retrospection

Erwin bounced flatly in the gutter, not himself flat, sitting upright, but the way his bottom "splatted" w/o resonating up life, was, like flat.

What? That is the word that lays ready to up. What? As if he you didn't, &c.

This time it was the electricity. The whole house now turned into a shifting shadow.

In the ersatz modernism, most things, even ourselves, are tied to electricity. So w/o it everything decamps & sits, flat, like a tire or a debunked idea.

Of which he was his own, as we suppose "others" (his idea) must be. So we say, sometimes, if we are social naturally & thoughtful, however.

Flat. Like they say, "Kicked to the curb." But now, even worse, to roll, or been thrust off & flattened. Not flat across the street, arms akimbo, like the imaginary dead.

"On yr ass," the Blood wd say. Or, "On yr ass." OK.

I guess we all know that, or that is the disposition.

Why? How? And them. My man Morris wd say, "And then, so what?" A challenge.

The question remains. Remains, like stays, longer a verb. Hold to that. (Can *that* be a verb? *That*? That it sticks—what about *Thating*?) Yeh, he was down there Thating.

Why is a long, wrinkled & circular Thating—to get to that—yeh, "Get to That!" Monk had another flatting for Thating.

So How always the trail. Without yr self out front, like if you got reversed, the self after the "I," then that's a woe—a woeing. (Read here, *Trial*.)

Since Woe, if it is not tossed out like a leaflet, is simply where.

The gutter or rolled off the curb Dig Dog, is to only that *is-ing* is stopped.

A dog off the sidewalk is that it where the dog be. Curb. Stop. If it was deeper you'd just slide around w/o necessarily that finger on the string that nots. Knots.

Bird sd, "You've hurt my friend, you cur!" & what did the Nabs "think"?

"What is that African-American gentleman referring to?"

That's why Bird cd be inside his stomach, like on the earth, itself cooking. And cooked, sadly.

He never got busted, you dig, of all of his "worthy constituents," except for that guile, of which the leaders' guidon speaks (given open dimension to guide).

But his life took no fifth, except the notes, & his curb was early extinction from the death ray of Jimmy Dorsey on television. (They say *The Ed Sullivan Show* massacred many unsuspecting artists, whose hearts were swallowed by cathode poisoning, made lethal with electronic corn!)

I was a He then, when looking at you flat—like the end of a page. The over the edge & following a shape.

How is you? meant silence, intent on misty mind condiment & edgeless afternoon in skull notation.

So woe is the number cd not tell you the dagger of they ugly was to waste them now.

My where from life wear as if this low that was my ware. Ob cos. Distress is a number.

Bipolar pain. Cold Bread. How the substance of the inside feeds. Go out, oh blowing Sun. Find the each of all the unending circle of is.

And him, still flat, trying to remember the touching interior of why he before was other than this Thating flat. A search. A quest lit with reality—terrible name, this place. Sound thrown as chance, head beat ing of under standing. Get up then. Blow that note. Be its endless substance. An us.

Listening to what is an image you won't look at, doing this inside. OK, glance & the thin wire of revulsion familiar, common as laughter, runs through yr attention.

Jesus, for instance, we'd say. The Negro babbling or co-babbling w/the host.

2000

The Pig Detector

"Hey, you know that dude I told you about?"

"The dude with the Rhythm Travel machine?"

"Yeh, yeh. Well, he invented a police exposure light ray, or something. You shine it on a person, and if they the police, the machine lights up and plays the first chords of 'I'll Be Glad When You're Dead, You Rascal You.'"

"Yeh?" was me responding.

"Yeh." Then we went out to a meeting so he could prove it.

"Yeh, no kidding, man." What weird otherness this brother comes up with. Can you remember the parade of Outechnology my man came up with? And let me tell you, all that dooba-dooba is somewhere out here operating.

"So what you gonna do with it? I wish you'd tell me what you did with the other whatnot."

"Hey, I'm thinking. But I sure ain't giving away what don't need to be gove away."

"Then why you tell me? Why you bring me here and almost lay this shit out?"

"You the Under-On community-relations mouth. *La Boca Grande Negra*."

"You speak Spanish?"

"I could."

"You wanna give it to some black organizations?"

"Probably to a few. Those that'll keep it under. You know, there's an Over and an Under."

"Legal and illegal."

"Yeabo! And you got to keep the connections quiet, the Who-Do, even if you running the existence. Because I take that as propaganda that let people know there's an Ultra Blue technology out here getting ready to Bop."

This dude laugh like Billy Eckstine's Big Band. "Yeh, Under-On. But—" Was he pausing or did he leave the room?

"But what?"

"Well, I'm always into another wrinkle of the out, the further out, and the gone."

"Dig that, the gone." That "gone" sound like James Brown screaming!

"I'm getting ready to add a mental disorientator or a body disorientator." He sound like Stevie now. "Put some doo-doo in the game."

That last riff had a tune to it too. Can't remember it. Maybe like "Pastime Paradise."

"What you mean?"

"The mental D.O. makes them start dropping dimes on each other. Get the real uglies busted. Taping each other, killer cops getting flicks, phone conversations. Suddenly confessing and throwing the evidence on the table in the middle of trials. Divulging police murders, beatings, scams, and shams." Now he was laughing like Marvin on "Mickey's Monkey."

"Yeh, yeh." You know me, I was dancing to the conversation. "What the other thing gonna do? The body-jammy?"

"Well . . ." he got a kind of sheepish look, maybe like the dude on *What Becomes of the Broken Hearted?* "First . . ." This was drawn out like a game-show host. *Furrrst!* Like that. "First, I was just gonna deconstruct they bodies and send them to expensive restaurants, but my conscience got in it."

"Oh yeah, what it tell you?" He was handing me my coat.

"Well, it ain't told me nothing yet. I just got a head-ring. The channel ain't come all the way in yet."

He was laughing when I split. Bending over his heebie-jeebie with a cold blue passion. *Expensive restaurants*, what that mean? We got to go down the street to Dick & Judy's every day?

December 2000

Post- and Pre-Mortem Dialogue

Suppose, I said to someone who I am close to, that the Saudis were the handled in this 9/11 business.

Oh?

And suppose, since most of the so-called terrorists were alleged to be Saudis—except for the ones who were never there, given the Identity Theft, like the dudes in Pakistan and Saudi who never left.

Yeh.

And suppose, as a quid pro from the Yanks moving out of Saudi, since it was getting a bit too hot, with the real Muslims chafing at Israel and the penetration of the Infidel all up in Saudi. The Seven Sisters. The deep crème-filled corruption of the Saudi Royal House.

Uh-huh. Like the stories about them 400 princes and no princesses and how they still dig boy, not scag either.

I'm gonna laugh before I tell you.

Tell me about the thirty-percent ownership of New York—at least the Plaza Hotel. The dude offered how many Negroes to 666, Giuliani, who refused on top cause under was sweeter?

Uh-huh.

And we know about how they all was in San Diego (living in La Jolla, Nixon's Disneyland for tiring mice &

ducks). The airplane lessons. Just take-off and banking, no landing.

Yeh.

And the obvious dung smell, like finding a terrorist passport in the ashes in front of the Twin Towers.

To where? Out?

And the rest of the BS. Change flight plans, no challenge from radio, no radio contact, no interceptors, Boston to World Trade Center to Pentagon.

The most carefully guarded strip of land on the planet.

Yeh.

And the weird stock-tinkering pullouts from American and United a month before.

The Israelis booking, the warnings. Sharon's un-visit. Your boy, Night Fighter Brown from Frisco.

By Way of Deception, the dude from the Mossad's book. About the 1st little 9/11 in the garage where the Palestinian went for the nooky and got popped instead of the Mossad nookyteer.

Yeh, I dig. But what?

Suppose the Saudis, in exchange for yr savage uncle booking. They in Qatar now. And with the Israeli thing. The promise to clean out Afghanistan, Palestine.

Transfer, they call it.

Saddam.

Yeh. Bush's old man gave him the stuff. They coulda checked the receipts.

Yeh.

Bush, the father, was Osama's roadie in the black gold trade. Cowboy baptized the Taliban to waste the Pink Afghan number.

What you saying?

Saying the Cowboy need a Pearl Harbor like his man Schicklgruber need the Reichstag, so they let the dogs out. Ate commies, union people, most heavy on the Jews!

Yeh, yeh. Reichstag Enablement Act, where yr man Asscraft come down. I see a big pink hiney sailing through the air, doing number one and number two on the whole world.

They think if they can doo-doo on everybody or get the E.P.A. to declare pee-pee-heavy weather, they can turn everybody into niggers!

Oh yeh. You mean, they be able to sing and dance and get fucked with on the highway?

Oh, there you come.

That's some out shit.

But this, if it was the Saudis playing Hitrabs for the Cowboy, the Cowboy can put on them black suits they got in the back of they closet.

And nut out on the whole whirl. Even change French fries to O'Reilly spuds. Get little Colon to take everything off the air. Let Murdoch do his no-place-to-go routine. It's all evil, except who telling you and I been converted to heathen!

You mean, on 9/11 the cops really did come?

And going to cop, everybody! Down on yr hands and needs new and old Negroes, we is gonna teach you about the rapture. Like they be sailing through the air with Jesus on the lead horse, just like in *Birth of a Nation* with a World War One.

Naw, updated. World War Two helmet.

You dig?

Afghanistan, Palestine, Iraq. Then Iran, Syria. Then a deep breath—it's off to see the Wizard.

The Yellow Brick Road. Right up to where the Key Maker in Matrix Deuce be hanging with the Keys to the entrance into meta-super-master. All y'all world is niggers now, and it ain't gonna be quitting time (like in *Gone with the Wind*) for a long never . . .

China.

Shit, do Cowboy know a billion motherfuckers up there? A bunch of which wd love his ass to ride up there so that they can turn that motherfucker into chopsticks.

And North Korea, the practice?

Shit, that ain't practice. That's nonsense.

It ain't to a fool. A fool think foolishness is good sense.

Anyway, if the Saudis was the hit nigras, so the Cowboy can move his doo-doo out. And give the boy-poppers a little room in they money.

Florida, San Diego, Koran in Boston airport. All of them Saudis & Bush and Israel and the Brits, who is always down for ugly.

Ain't that where the Devil first hit when he left the Pole?

So you saying the Cowboy, the Saudis, the Israel, and John Bull's one-nut kin is the actual doo-doo?

Straight out of the Cowboy Bible. With Jesus sailing down through the clouds to ice the Jews as soon as Israel free from the Colored.

Dig that. You don't believe FDR pulled a choo-choo with Pearl Harbor too?

Hey, I didn't see the movie.

But I saw *Matrix* Deuce where they living in Zion.

Do that make them Zionists?

I saw where the French dude was the villain and was keeping the Chinaman locked up cause he had the key.

The French-Chinese trade.

Historic. I seen that weird flick where the same dude in *Matrix*—his name ain't Kneel or Neil—it's Neo.

You mean they left the "GR" out?

Yeh, like you leave the Are out in yr man's title, he is then suddenly a fiend!

Gotcha. OK, OK.

So.

I suppose to say, "So." So?

They coming back another gin. New World Order. Homeland Security. Shock and Awe! Like the Concentration Camps was just Slave Plantations for Jews and other uncools.

So the Arab is the Jew this twirl?

Yeh, but dig, brother. You look like an Arab. Yr boy say he an original Jew, and we all know all y'all very colored.

Yeh. So what we supposed to do?

Get busy, is what. All us need to get busy.

Very busy!

(*All leave.*)

June 12, 2003
Brick City, New Ark

Also from AKASHIC BOOKS

BECOMING ABIGAIL by Chris Abani
*Essence Magazine Book Club selection
*A *New York Times* Editor's Choice
128 pages, trade paperback, $11.95

"Compelling and gorgeously written, this is a coming-of-age novella like no other. Chris Abani explores the depths of loss and exploitation with what can only be described as a knowing tenderness. An extraordinary, necessary book."
—Cristina Garcia, author of *Dreaming in Cuban*

IRON BALLOONS
HIT FICTION FROM JAMAICA'S CALABASH WRITER'S WORKSHOP
edited by Colin Channer
282 pages, trade paperback, $14.95

CONTRIBUTORS: Colin Channer, Marlon James, Elizabeth Nunez, Kwame Dawes, Kaylie Jones, Geoffrey Philp, Rudolph Wallace, Konrad Kirlew, Alwin Bully, A-dZiko Simba, and Sharon Leach.

"Channer's story, and the others he has collected, is raw and uncensored. [It] comes at you with hurricane force and an irresistible title . . . and is something of a tour de force."
—*New York Times*

JOHN CROW'S DEVIL by Marlon James
*A *New York Times* Editor's Choice
232 pages, hardcover, $19.95

"A powerful first novel . . . Writing with assurance and control, James uses his small-town drama to suggest the larger anguish of a postcolonial Jamaican society struggling for its own identity."
—*New York Times*

SOUTHLAND by Nina Revoyr
*A *Los Angeles Times* bestseller
*Winner of a Lambda Literary Award
348 pages, trade paperback, $15.95

"What makes a book like *Southland* resonate is that it merges elements of literature and social history with the propulsive drive of a mystery, while evoking Southern California as a character, a key player in the tale."
—*Los Angeles Times*

BRONX BIANNUAL: ISSUE NO. 1
edited by Miles Marshall Lewis
184 pages, trade paperback, $14.95

CONTRIBUTORS: Adam Mansbach, KRS-One, Donnell Alexander, Greg Tate, Caille Millner, muMs, Michael A. Gonzales, Reginald Lewis, and others.

"A truly bi-coastal melting pot of hip-hop culture and ideas."
—*Elemental Magazine*

ADIOS MUCHACHOS
by Daniel Chavarría
Winner of a 2001 Edgar Award
245 pages, trade paperback, $13.95

"Daniel Chavarría has long been recognized as one of Latin America's finest writers. Now he again proves why . . ."
—William Heffernan